ANOTHER FUNERAL

greenhill

ANOTHER FUNERAL

a novella

BRUCE J LEES

(✳) **green**hill

https://greenhillpublishing.com.au/

Lees, Bruce J (author)
Another Funeral
ISBN 978-1-923088-16-0
FICTION

Typeset Calluna 10.5/16
Cover and book design by Green Hill Publishing

For Collette

CHAPTER ONE

'So how did you know Donald?' the old bloke asked him just as Larry reached for a sandwich. His ill-fitting sleeve dusted some lettuce trimmings off the edge of the platter.

'His late wife was a friend of Maggie, me missus.'

'Really? She died absolutely years ago.'

Where was Maggie? She had left him by himself to go to the loo. The death notice had said Donald's wife was deceased, but how was he supposed to know it was years ago? He hated this bit. Maggie was the one who could bullshit her way out of anything. She was the one who had turned on the waterworks at Vinnies, resulting in them both being fitted out in their funeral outfits for next to nothing.

His dark suit was not the best fit in the world. The sleeves were too long. Maggie's grey skirt and navy jacket looked pretty good on her, although the cream blouse was starting to look a bit grubby. She had a sauce stain from yesterday's funeral that she had tried to sponge out.

'I can't remember the exact details; she was pretty upset.' Larry popped the triangular sandwich into his mouth.

Surely the old bugger wouldn't expect him to speak with his mouth full.

'I'd known Donald since high school. He was my dearest friend.' Tears welled up in the old man's eyes and slid down amongst the folds in his weathered face.

Boy this was getting tricky. Where was Maggie?

'I am very sorry for your loss.' Larry fell back on this standard line he used many times before. It was times like this that he felt just a little guilty about gate crashing funerals. But a feed is a feed.

He looked around and saw Maggie on the other side of the room at the urn getting a second cup of tea.

'Excuse me, I had better check on the wife,' he said as he abandoned his teary new friend.

He weaved his way through the mourners to reach Maggie just as she took a bite out of a lamington, coconut showering her stained blouse.

'You just about ready to leave?' he whispered in her ear.

'Are you full already? I haven't finished me cuppa.' She reached out for a piece of chocolate hedgehog.

'I thought I was going to get sprung,' he said as he glanced over at the funeral director talking to what must have been Donald's granddaughter. A pretty young thing, it was she who had delivered the eulogy. 'I reckon we should POQ. How's your handbag? '

'I've gotta couple of sausage rolls and some of those yummy little cakes.' Maggie patted her handbag gently. She finished the rest of her tea and dropped the hedgehog into her open handbag. 'Come on then, if you really want to go, we can.'

They manoeuvred their way to the door only to come face to face with the pretty granddaughter.

'You did a wonderful job,' Larry mumbled as she leaned forward and gave him a hug. He held her tight for a second or two. That was a bonus.

'Thank you for coming,' she said giving Maggie a cursory hug.

With that, they stepped out through the door onto Queens Parade and scanned the street for a tram.

'So, what's it going to be? Back to home sweet home or the library?' Larry relied on Maggie for the most important decisions.

Maggie smiled at him. Home sweet home was currently a squat in Collingwood. A terrace house surrounded by that temporary fencing as it waited for demolition.

'I really need the library's internet to Google that Richard Nelson whose funeral is tomorrow. See what I can find out and work what story we can spin at that one. Not too sure how we can get out to Brighton. I hate using the trains.'

The trains were much harder to use without a Myki card, unless you picked stations without physical barriers you were required to pass through. If you had to touch on or off with your prepaid card to enter or leave a station, you were in trouble and a free ride was difficult. Trams were much easier, as long as you kept your eyes peeled for those sneaky inspectors with those bum bags around their bellies. They generally hunted in packs of three or so. Larry was good at looking ahead and spotting any, allowing them to alight from the tram before they were caught travelling without paying.

'I reckon anybody from Brighton should provide a pretty good spread.' Larry chuckled in anticipation 'There is a tram stop on the next corner. An eighty-six will get us close to the Fitzroy Library, or should we hoof it and walk off some of those sausage rolls?'

'We'll take the tram. Could be in for a bit of a walk tomorrow.' Maggie linked her arm with Larry as they headed towards the tram stop.

CHAPTER TWO

Maggie struggled to get to sleep. Larry was gently snoring beside her on the mattress in the centre of the floor of the front room. She was not altogether convinced making the trip out to the Brighton funeral was a good idea. She had done her research. It was really a memorial service following an earlier cremation, so that was a plus. The luncheon would be served straight after the service. It was going to be a bit difficult to get there as, the funeral home was about two kilometres from the railway station. In addition, going by train meant they would probably have to put a couple of dollars on the Senior Myki cards they had stashed away for emergencies. Perhaps the sensible thing to do would be to spend those few dollars on a sandwich to share or some hot chips.

There had been no wait for internet use at the library and Google had been informative about the deceased. It seems he had been a company director of an accounting firm and was most likely worth a shitload. He had owned a few racehorses over the years including one called *Rainbow Spring* which had won a few group one races. On that basis they could probably claim that they knew him through his racing connections. He was survived by three daughters; the death notice in the paper had supplied their names.

It certainly looked like a good opportunity to get their main feed for the day, perhaps even a drink thrown in, but it was a long way from their usual stomping ground and just a bit beyond their comfort zone. Maggie tossed around the pros and cons until eventually she fell into a restless sleep.

The sound of the garbage truck roaring between the bins lined up in the street woke Larry. He quietly cursed himself. He had meant to slip out last night and place their week's rubbish in a neighbour's bin. The last thing they needed was the smell of the week's garbage adding to the musty damp odours that already permeated the whole house. Just because they were living in a squat without electricity and only cold water didn't mean they didn't try to keep things clean. Things weren't too bad for the time being.

Apparently, the demolition of the tiny weatherboard house had been objected to on heritage grounds. The corrugated iron roof was rusted and leaked like the treasurer's office before budget night. Someone had stolen the cast iron lacework that decorated the front veranda, the front wall had been tagged by some prick with a spray-can and the whole house seem to be sinking on the southern side. As far as Larry was concerned, the derelict ruin needed pulling down, but for the moment it provided the pair of them with a place to stay.

They had been in the house for four weeks and had tried to keep a low profile. So far none of the neighbours had caused them any trouble, although some of them must have been aware of squatters living in the condemned house. Hard garbage left on the street before the council pick up had allowed them to scrounge the mattress, a card table and two plastic chairs. The rest of their belongings were stored in a couple of large striped plastic storage bags and one suitcase Larry had kept from his former life.

They had cleaned up the kitchen. Well, it was a bit of a stretch to call it a kitchen. There was a stainless-steel sink and a small Laminex benchtop over some dilapidated cupboards. The doors were missing from one set of overhead cupboards and there was an empty space for a refrigerator. No hot water, although the cold tap was still working, allowing them to wash the few dishes they had picked up from an op shop for twenty cents apiece. The ritual of rinsing the dishes gave a domestic overtone to their hovel. One cupboard had proved mouse-proof, in which they stored their dishes and food. Still, they couldn't cook at all without gas or electricity, but the plates made take-aways or the treasures from Maggie's handbag seem a little more like a meal.

Larry shivered, rolled over and spooned Maggie; it was amazing how much heat such a delicate body could generate. Despite his efforts over the last year, this was the extent of their intimacy. Maggie had resisted any attempts by Larry to move their relationship beyond bedtime cuddles. She was a woman with significant baggage from a past life. Larry too had a past life best forgotten.

It was too early to get out of bed, even if his stomach disagreed.

Maggie stirred. 'I heard your stomach growling,' she muttered.

'Would you like me to get you a couple of Weet-Bix and you could have breakfast in bed?' Hunger was getting the better of him.

'That would be lovely, but you'd better give the milk the sniff test. I don't want anything if the milks off.'

Larry rolled out of bed and trailed down the damp hallway to the kitchen to prepare breakfast. It wasn't much, things were tight. The unemployment benefit that Larry received amounted to $40 a day and that spread between the two of them didn't go far. Thank goodness he still had a bank account and an on-line MyGov account, so Centrelink was unaware of his homeless status. He was only six months away from turning sixty-six and he was looking forward to the day as he would then be eligible for the age pension. If only he could convince Maggie to register at Centrelink to receive some benefits things would be better. There was no way she would allow her name to be listed anywhere, on any data-base. Fear of her ex-husband had morphed into paranoia.

He made his way back to the front room, dodging the strategically placed empty paint can and buckets which caught the drips that fell from the heavens. He carried the two bowls of cereal with all the finesse of a waiter on his very first shift. 'Madam, your breakfast as ordered.'

Maggie sat up, brushed her fading red hair from her eyes and gave Larry that smile which kept him sane. 'Thank you, kind sir,' she replied as she pulled back the covers to allow the waiter into her bed.

As Larry ate his cereal, his mind wandered back to their difficult circumstances. Once he received the pension life could only improve, although his chance of getting govern-ment housing was close to zero. Currently there was no way they could afford any rental accommodation and this current squat was a godsend, much better than living on the street or in Larry's car. The beat-up Ford Laser car had long since disappeared from his life. He couldn't afford the registration or having it repaired when it finally gave up the ghost. It had eventually been towed away by the council. It was a shock the day when it had disappeared, cutting the last of his ties to the past.

CHAPTER THREE

FIVE YEARS EARLIER 2014

'The court appreciates the fact that you, Larry Jenkins, have pleaded guilty to the charges and have expressed some remorse. However, your crime is not one that can be regarded as anything less than a serious breach of trust of your employer and a blatant surrendering to greed and dishonesty. The court recognises that you may have not been the ringleader and you were too easily led by your co-accused in this swindle. Nevertheless, it was you who paid out on the false invoices knowing that they were for work and materials that did not exist. White collar crime is still a crime.'

Larry didn't like the sound of the beak's summation.

'You are hereby sentenced to five years imprisonment and must serve three before being eligible for parole.'

Larry turned around to look amongst the onlookers hoping to see his wife Jenny in tears. She was there alright, but there were no tears. Her eyes were full of disgust and were enough to make Larry turn away.

It had been a different story when he was flush with funds from his first dive into the crime pool. All smiles then. She was more than happy with the flash beach side town house he bought in Williamstown. They had both been on cloud nine and she had even given up working at Myer in the city. No more standing all day on her feet in the home-wares department. She had joined a gym, taken up tennis and was pretty fit for a woman in her mid-fifties. Larry had kept working as a bookkeeper for Appleton Constructions before his involvement in the scam had been discovered.

'Come on Mr Jenkins, time to take you to the cells. Just place your hands behind your back please.' The handcuffs bit into Larry's wrists as the officer wasted no time in securing his prisoner.

'Christ mate, do you really think I'm about to do a runner? Don't I get to say goodbye to the wife?'

Larry turned around again to the body of the court-room just in time to see Jennifer pass through the door with Marcus, his solicitor. She had turned up the collar of her cashmere jacket, tied her silk scarf over her blond hair and had put on her Ray-Ban sunglasses; was she trying to disguise herself?

The guard led him downstairs from the dock and along a poorly lit corridor to the cells. Here he surrendered his belt and tie and sat on the bench set against one wall. Another bloke was dozing on the bench on the other side of the cell dressed in jeans and tee shirt. Larry figured he must have been well over six foot tall and covered in tattoos. How was a weedy little guy like himself going to survive in jail?

The big guy's eyes opened. 'Me name's Mick. How long ya get?'

'Bloody five fucking years. Jesus, some child molesters get less. I didn't hurt nobody.' Larry was having trouble holding it together.

'You'll be right mate. They will end up sending you to some soft joint like Golden Hills if it was just fiddling the books not fiddling with kids.' Mick chuckled at his own joke.

'Me solicitor reckons they'll seize me house 'cause it was purchased with the proceeds of crime. I reckon they're punishing me twice.' Larry saw this as really unjust and so did the missus, hence the evil eye in the courtroom. 'So, what's your story Mick?'

'Got done for grievous bodily harm. Bastard deserved it though. Ran off with the wife.'

'Oh,' said Larry nodding his head. The pit of his stomach tightened just a little more; he was going to have to get used to mixing with a new crowd.

Mick's prediction turned out to be true. After a month in the city, Larry was assessed as being of low risk and was transported up to Golden Hills, a minimum-security prison near

Bendigo, in northern Victoria.

Larry couldn't believe his luck. When he stepped out of the prison van it was just on sunset. Before him was a huge mansion illuminated by the setting sun. Behind and around this beautiful piece of history from the late 1800's were numerous outbuildings. Beyond the buildings were orchards, gardens and open countryside. Larry heard the occasional bellowing of cows from the prison's dairy herd. The air was filled with botanical smells, far removed from the stink of bodily odours that had dominated his incarceration so far. Even the kookaburras some distance away were laughing at Larry's good fortune; things were looking up.

For the first two weeks he was sleeping in a cell, before he was allocated to a cottage which housed five fellow inmates. Most of the blokes seemed pretty normal, although there were a few Larry was warned to avoid. After being assigned to the wood products factory, he soon found his niche. His computer bookkeeping skills were put to use in keeping records of the inventory of materials and the various products produced by the enterprise.

The prison officers were a mixed bag. They seemed pretty keen on everybody getting along and there were even some women amongst them. These women were popular, as were a couple of women among the instructors who came into the prison to run educational courses. These could be undertaken after your work shifts. Courses were supposed to help you when you were released, but some guys took them just to hear a woman's voice.

Margot, a middle-aged teacher with a sultry voice, came from the TAFE College in Bendigo and ran a computer class on Monday and Wednesday afternoons. Larry signed up as this was his bread and butter. Quite a few of the men were a bit taken by Margot and hence her classes were filled to capacity and pretty busy.

Margot soon sussed him out. 'This is too easy for you isn't it, Larry? If you are going to be here, then you had better act like my assistant and help these blokes.'

'Sure, no trouble, Ms Warren.'

'What are you like with spreadsheets Larry?'

'Piece of piss; sorry, what I meant to say is I'm pretty good with them.'

Margot giggled. 'That's great because they're not my strongpoint. You could be a real help.'

And so began Larry's side hustle as a tutor in the computer class. He was kind of proud when he gained the nickname *Prof* in recognition of him being regarded as a smart bloke. There's a first time for everything. Things could have been so much worse.

Larry heard little from the outside. He received only the one letter from Jennifer, telling him the Sheriff's Office had forced her to vacate the townhouse and it was put up for auction. As his solicitor had warned him, it was claimed it had been bought with the proceeds of crime. Larry knew that this was not entirely true, as a small amount of money he had inherited from his parents was also invested in the house. Jenny said she'd had enough, wanted a divorce and was moving to Queensland to be with her sister. There was little he could do other than write to her to say he was sorry about the townhouse. Her response to the whole business had hurt and it was not long before any love left slipped away to be replaced with a bitterness, he didn't know he was capable of.

Three years would soon pass.

CHAPTER FOUR

'Can't be too much longer,' Larry whispered in Maggie's ear.

By this stage of the service, they were showing a pictorial record of Richard Nelson's life or Uncle Dick as the nephew given the eulogy had called him. They had some really nice classical music playing in the background, which Larry remembered from the good old days when he could enjoy such things. What was the composer's name? Alan Copland? No, Aaron, that's right, Aaron Copland; *Appalachian Spring*.

Larry suddenly stopped thinking about the music with a start. He found himself staring at a picture of the recently departed Dick with his arm around *Henry the Hammer* from Golden Hills. His other hand was holding the reins of a racehorse. Boy, is it ever a small world! So far, he had avoided any contact with past acquaintances from his time spent inside.

The photo presentation finished and the MC moved to the lectern and addressed everybody seated in the chapel and those standing behind. The crowd had spilled out into the foyer of the funeral home.

'Now I asked everyone to join the family for refreshments in the reception room just through those doors and help celebrate Richard's life. I need to let you know that it was one of our friend's dying wishes that he didn't want tears as he had enjoyed his life and to feel free to have a good time at his expense. The family would like to thank you one and all for coming today.'

Maggie and Larry followed the crowd. Maggie was glad they had managed to get two of the last seats in the back row, as they had had walked a couple of kilometres from Brighton Station. Her funeral pumps weren't up for too much walking. How her feet screamed for her worn cross trainers.

The reception room had a large rectangular table with a variety of finger foods spread from one end to the other. To one side was an urn with cups set up for guests to help themselves to tea or coffee. In addition, a couple of waiters carried trays around with tall glasses of sparkling wine and open bottles of Crown Lager. Larry's spirits lifted and his concerns about meeting up with Henry diminished. It was not that Henry was a bad fellow; in fact they had shared a few classes in prison. Henry at the time had assured him it helped you get parole to be seen to be improving yourself.

Armed with a Crownie and a pastry shell filled with some sort of seafood, he guided Maggie to a quiet spot against the wall.

'You must try one of these Maggie.'

'Nothing wrong with these sandwiches and the cham-pagne's awesome.' Maggie was pleased they had made the effort of coming.

'I'm getting another, I'll get one for you.' Larry made his way to the central table.

He had no sooner loaded up his plate when there was a crash of dishes, quite a kerfuffle, followed by a scream.

'Help! Somebody help! Is there a doctor here? Anybody know CPR?'

'*Shit. That's me*,' thought Larry who had completed a first aid course at Golden Hills. He was dithering, hoping someone would step forward, when he felt a tap on the shoulder. He turned to see Henry the Hammer behind him.

'Come on Prof, that's us mate, you remember? I'll do the chest bit you give him a bit of air.'

What could he do? He joined Henry kneeling on the floor beside a bloke in his forties already losing colour. Henry had already checked his mouth and rolled the unconscious mourner onto his back.

'Give him a couple of breaths when I get to 30,' Henry barked before he started chest compressions on the poor man. 'One, two, three,' and on he went. Larry was not looking forward to what was to come next trying to recall what he had done with the dummy torso in first aid class.

'.......twenty nine, thirty. Go on Prof, give him a couple.'

Larry tilted back the man's bald head, pinched his nose, placed his mouth over the blue lips and blew. Sure enough his patient's chest rose. Larry took another breath and repeated this unnatural act. His mind ran in circles as Henry started counting again with each compression. Urhh, it must be like kissing a bloke. Thirty came around once more and Larry did it all again.

They kept repeating the cycle for hours; well, it seemed like hours, but was probably only ten minutes before they heard the ambulance siren heading down the Nepean Highway. Two paramedics took over and in just minutes found a pulse and the patient showed signs of consciousness. In no time they had him on oxygen, inserted a drip and he was loaded into the back of the ambulance.

Larry was stunned. Never in his lifetime had he ever done anything like this before. Poor old Henry looked a bit exhausted as they stood there staring at the departing ambulance. One of the funeral staff sidled up to the pair.

'So, what's it to be gentlemen, a beer or a cup of tea?'

'Couple of beers thanks, luv. That was quite a workout.' Once again Henry took control.

The cold beer washed Larry's mouth of the strange taste left after all that mouth-to-mouth stuff with another man. 'I better check on Maggie.'

'You had better introduce me,' said Henry as he followed Larry back to the edge of the room.

'Henry this is Maggie,' he didn't say wife as he normally did when they were playing their roles 'Maggie, this is Henry, a mate of mine from a few years ago.'

An ashen Maggie held out her hand and shook the big man's hand. She couldn't believe what had taken place and was shocked that Larry had exposed himself so publicly when they always tried to keep a low profile. A funeral staff member bought more drinks.

'More beer gentlemen? Another Prosecco ma'am?'

Suddenly they seemed to have celebrity status. Maggie took a gulp of the fresh glass of Prosecco.

'I think we should go soon Larry, dear.'

She felt it was getting all too complicated. Anymore beer and Larry will spill the beans to this dodgy looking mate. They had never met someone they knew at a funeral before. Maggie did not want to be anywhere near the centre of attention; the whole idea of their shenanigans was to keep in the shadows. In all the time she had been with Larry, he had never done anything like this.

'No way, little lady, we have to catch up, the Prof and me,' demanded Henry.

Maggie gave him a look to kill but all she got in return was a cheesy grin and a wink. God, she hated big men who thought their mere presence let them rule the roost.

'So, tell me Prof, who's related to the late Dick, you or the pretty Maggie here? I aint ever seen you at the track with Dick, so you can't have been a mate.'

Larry looked at Maggie hoping she could invent something quickly. Their story had been to claim they knew Richard Nelson through racing circles. That wasn't going to work.

'Well, you see.' Larry was stalling hoping for a miracle.

'I'm a cousin of his first wife,' mumbled Maggie trying desperately to recall the name she had read on- line. She remembered he had been married twice from her research."

'Oh that bitch,' Henry blurted out, 'Sorry, no offense intended. You can't choose your relatives, can you, sweetie?' Another wink.

Maggie was taking a distinct dislike to this oaf. 'Larry, we better get going. We don't want to get caught in the rain.'

'What? You're not driving? What happened Prof? You blow over o-five?' queried Henry.

'Don't have a car anymore.' Larry looked pleadingly at Maggie hoping she could explain.

'Parking's too much of a problem where we live,' she came up with.

'Know what you mean. I can give you a lift after we have had a few more bevies, besides I am sure you will want to catch up with the family.'

They had more drinks. More drinks than Larry and Maggie were used to and numerous people came and thanked the men for their heroic action. It seems the gentleman they saved was a bookie who had become mates with the deceased at the track. There seemed a suggestion that he may have been a bit dodgy, although nobody actually came out and said as much.

Later, as they climbed into Henry's well-worn BMW, he asked where they lived and without thinking Larry blurted out the street name of their current abode. Maggie sank further into the back seat. How could this have all gone tits up? They had been doing so well just the two of them with this funeral lark.

When they entered Heather Street and were just a hundred metres from their squat, they came to a block of red brick flats built sometime in the 1940s. 'Just here, thanks Henry. Our flat is out the back of the block,' Maggie said.

Puzzlement swept across Larry's face for a moment or two before he muttered. 'Thanks mate. Bloody good of you to give us a lift.'

'Least I could do for you Prof. I will give you me mobile number.' He handed Larry a card as they got out of the BMW. 'You look after him won't ya, luv.' He gave Maggie another of those lecherous winks.

Once the car had left, they hurried down the street to their squat surrounded by the tall temporary fencing. They entered an adjacent lane that led them around to the back gate.

What a day! An extensive review of things was in order.

CHAPTER FIVE

TWO YEARS EARLIER 2017

'Where's Maggie this morning Debra?' Faye kept a record of attendance although nobody knew why.

'I rang her this morning to see if she wanted a lift, but she said she felt crook.' Debra looked around the group of women who made up the book club, wondering who else shared her suspicions about what was going on in the Bennington household. She glanced over at Amanda who rolled her eyes.

'Well, we are nearly all here. Now who's ready to talk about *Olive Kitteridge?*' said Faye, as the rest of the group nodded their heads in agreement.

Later, outside in the library's carpark Amanda ambled over to Debra, her tent like kaftan catching the breeze. She leant against Debra's Subaru, challenging its suspension. 'Well, what do you reckon about Maggie, Debs? I hope that bastard of a husband hasn't been thumping her again.' Amanda always called a spade a spade.

'She did claim when she had her broken arm, it was an accident. You can't do much if she won't tell.' Debra didn't want to cause trouble for her friend Maggie, but she had her doubts about the broken arm that was accompanied by facial bruising.

'Bullshit, if you ask me.' Amanda was forthcoming with her opinion. 'I think one of us should go and check on her. Do you think you could talk sense into her?'

'I'll give it a try,' replied Debra. 'I'll pop in on my way home and I will let you know.'

'Look, I've plenty of spare rooms at my place.' Amanda suggested and reached out to stroke Debra's arm. 'I can come with you if you want me to, but I reckon it might be best if it was just you.'

Debra had to agree. If Amanda was present, it would be difficult for Maggie to make her own decision.

Debra took a moment or two to catch her breath. It was quite a climb up a steep set of steps to reach Maggie's home perched high above the street. She knocked on the door for the third time before she heard footsteps and the door cracked open. Her worst fears were confirmed when she saw just enough of Maggie's face to tell that her husband Brian had been yet again using her as a punching bag.

'Let me in please Maggie,' she said as she pushed the door open and a badly battered Maggie stepped aside. 'You had better tell me what's been going on.'

Debra guided Maggie to the sofa in the front room. Maggie eventually stopped crying and between sobs explained. 'Brian lost his temper when I said I was planning to go to book club.'

'What's he got against book club?' Debra asked.

'He reckons you'll all put ideas in my head.' She let out a sob before continuing 'And if that wasn't bad enough, I was shaking so much I spilt some soup on his good work suit when I was serving up his dinner.'

Debra put her arm around her friend.

'He slapped me so hard I ended up on the kitchen floor and that was when he kicked me a couple of times. I said if he didn't stop, I'd leave him.'

'Oh Maggie, that's what you should do.'

'He went ballistic then. I thought my life was over when he had his hands around my throat. Said he'd kill me if I left. He apologised this morning and claimed he would never hurt me again. But he always says that.'

Debra, having been encouraged by Amanda knew she had to do something. 'I'll help you pack a few things Maggie, you have to leave him. I'll take you to Amanda's house. She'll put you up for a bit.'

'What if he finds me there? He'll go mental again. He'll kill me; I know he will. He's just as likely to bash Amanda as well.'

'We'll get an order from the cops that will say he can't come near you. Amanda knows all about that stuff.'

That proved to be so true. Amanda was a big help and had an intervention order in no time which was supposed to keep Brian away from Maggie. Even so, it was of little use as he somehow tracked her down to where she was staying with her friend.

Maggie peered through the crack in the bedroom door. She saw Amanda in the hallway, talking to Brian through the security screen door. It was less than 48 hours since the intervention order had been granted. It was hard to see Brian, as Amanda's rotund figure blocked the doorway making it difficult to see Brian's reaction.

Her voice was calm but firm. 'I know you want to talk to Maggie, but she has had enough.' She held up her mobile phone. 'You can't be anywhere near her and if you don't leave, I'll call the cops.'

'It's got nothing to do with you, you, interfering bitch!' shouted Brian as he tugged at the screen door. 'She's my wife, I only want a word or two.'

'Go away please,' said Amanda as she keyed in triple 0 and switched her phone to speaker mode. Anybody on the other end would get an earful of Brian's ranting. The dial tone incensed Brian, causing his yelling to go up a notch making it almost impossible for Maggie to hear what Amanda was saying on the phone.

'Maggie come out here right now or you'll be sorry!' he screamed trying to wrench open the door. That was enough. Maggie could feel her heart thumping in her chest and she moved further back into the room trembling with fear. She decided the best thing she could do would be to go into hiding. Her friend Amanda shouldn't be put at risk. She started planning.

Brian had moved around the back of the house and was pounding his shoulder against the back door by the time the two burly police officers arrived. He had almost succeeded, as the lock's strike plate had loosened on the doorframe. In no time they had him handcuffed and dragged him out to the street.

It was all too much for Maggie and she decided the best thing she could do would be leave Sydney altogether. Early one morning, she snuck out of Amanda's house leaving a note for her friend, explaining her need to go into hiding. She had managed to withdraw a little over a thousand dollars from an ATM using the credit card Brian allowed her to use for groceries. With this small kitty, she caught the train to Melbourne. She had the address of a women's refuge in Melbourne that a search on Amanda's old desktop computer had provided.

A constant stream of urgent cases arriving on the doorstep of the Flemington terrace house that served as a refuge, meant the three-week maximum stay was enforced. Maggie then discovered the best she could do for accommodation was a damp and depressing rooming house in Fitzroy.

Terrified that Brian would track her down, caused her to be stubborn and irrational, ignoring the help and advice provided at the refuge regarding getting assistance from Centrelink. There was no way she was going to allow her name to find its way onto any data base.

She had luckily found part-time work as a kitchen hand which had been advertised in the window of a little restaurant in Gertrude Street. Jack, a pimple faced kid of about eighteen, was given the task of showing her the ropes.

'So, you're our new dish pig? What does somebody old like you want to do this for?'

'Money Jack. It is not so easy to get a job,' Maggie paused before adding, 'for somebody old like me.'

'Sorry Maggie it's just everybody is young, if you know what I mean.' He had the decency to blush slightly. 'The sink over here is where we wash the saucepans and cooking stuff, the next one along is for the plates.'

'Why don't they have a machine?' Maggie enquired.

'Takes too bloody long the boss reckons. There is one behind the bar for the glasses, but you won't have to worry about that.'

'So, Jack, do I get to do anything other than wash dishes?'

Jack laughed. 'Ivan might let you peel some potatoes. He can be a cranky bastard.'

Ivan was the chef in charge and Maggie was warned about his temper tantrums. Maggie decided to keep her distance, as the last thing she needed was angry men in her life. No never again. Not ever again.

The weeks rolled by with just weekend shifts assigned to her. She felt really old amongst the rest of the cafe's workers who consisted almost entirely of students and backpackers. Standing on her feet for up to eight hours washing dishes, pots and pans made her feel every bit of her fifty-eight years of age. Her wages, paid in cash, barely covered the $100 per week for the room and her other day to day expenses. Her initial $1000 stake was almost gone.

CHAPTER SIX

ONE YEAR EARLIER 2018

Larry felt sorry for himself. He was reduced to this; a rooming house in Fitzroy at a hundred dollars a week. Life had been liveable since he had been granted parole. His supervisor had helped him get a job in a warehouse that seemed to stock a huge range of inexpensive products that came mainly from China.

When orders came in from cheap variety stores from all over Australia, he was one of three who set about gathering the products listed on the order. Using this *pick list*, he would locate the future bargains from the miles of shelving, add them to his trolley. When he had completed an order, he would stack it onto a pallet before another of his work mates shrunk wrapped the whole lot, pallet and all. Then he started all over again on a new order.

Larry didn't mind the work as each order was always a little different and all the walking was good exercise. It all came crashing down when one of the major chains *Only a Dollar or Two* went belly up and the liquidators were called in. The warehouse had to let staff go and adopted a last in first out policy. Larry was made redundant.

He managed to pay his rent on his tiny St Kilda studio apartment for the first month after his sacking. Securing employment when you are in your sixties with a criminal record proved to be impossible. Despite eventually qualifying for Centrelink's Newstart payment, he missed paying the next month's rent and was given a warning. Despite his efforts at frugality, he was faced with eviction.

So here he was in a flea pit in Fitzroy, trying to survive on about a hundred bucks a week after he had paid for his accommodation. The other tenants all had their problems as well. A sickly smell of marijuana smoke mixed with mould from damp and bad plumbing filled the air. The shared bathrooms and kitchen were worn and tired. The paint in the kitchen was peeling from the walls and the kitchen sink struggled to swallow the dish water after somebody actually washed dishes.

In the evening, at about six o'clock, Larry picked up his milk crate holding his food supplies and made his way downstairs to the kitchen. He rinsed out a saucepan, opened a can of baked beans and popped a couple of slices of stale bread in the toaster.

'Smells like somebody is cooking up a feast.'

Larry looked around to see a smiling face. That face

belonged to a woman, slight in build with hair trying to decide if it would stay red or surrender to grey. Her eyes were a beautiful blue, the sort of eyes that dominate a face and distract from the wrinkles and freckles.

'Sure, beans on toast,' he replied. 'Some feast.'

'You new here?'

'My first week. Hope to get myself sorted and not be here for too long.' Larry tried to sound confident, but knew getting a job was not likely, in fact it probably wasn't going to happen.

'That's always been my plan, but I've been stuck here for the best part of twelve months. By the way, my name's Maggie.'

'Do you want some of me beans? I really can't eat a whole can.' Larry couldn't believe he had made such a lame offer to this quite attractive woman. Attractive in a mature way; with a captivating smile and those blue eyes that just sparkled. They were eyes you could drown in.

'Thanks for the offer, Mr New Guy, but I really only came to make myself a cuppa.'

'Larry's the name. Sorry I ..umm....'

'Don't apologise, your offer was greatly appreciated,' she said as she plugged in the electric kettle. 'I could make you a cuppa if you have your tea black and don't mind sharing a tea bag.'

'Thanks, Maggie, that would be good.' Larry was not used to kindness coming from strangers.

'Actually, I might have a few beans if your offer is still

open.' Maggie could not believe her own behaviour. She had a deep-seated fear of most male members of the species, however Larry seemed like a real lost soul and pretty benign. Why, he had even blushed a little when he offered to share his dinner. She watched him as he dropped more bread in the toaster, then fossicked around in his milk crate and retrieved a tub of margarine.

In no time at all they were seated at the grubby kitchen table, dining on beans on toast, washed down with weak cups of Liptons. Maggie was surprised in herself; here she was actually feeling comfortable with a man for the first time in years. He seemed so harmless and had shown her a simple kindness.

Their paths did not cross for three days until on Saturday morning Larry found Maggie in the kitchen looking stressed. There were dark bags under those eyes and she was wearing a baggy tracksuit that looked too big on her slender frame.

'What's up Maggie? You don't look too happy?'

'I think I was given the sack last night from my job, as a kitchen hand, at that Italian place round the corner in Gertrude Street. They told me not to come in tonight. I think the chef has his eye on the Swedish backpacker that has had a few daytime shifts and he has allocated her my two lousy weekend spots,' Maggie explained. 'I half expect the same thing will happen to my Wednesday shift.'

'That's no good,' he said sympathetically.

'No good! It's a disaster. I need that money to pay for this dump.'

'You'll find something else,' he said.

'Not if I have to compete with leggy backpackers. How's your job hunting going?' She looked at him with raised eyebrows.

'No luck, but I am getting by on my dole payments. You should go to Centrelink and get on Newstart. You would be eligible I'm sure.'

She looked away and muttered. 'Can't do that.'

Larry had the good sense not to poke his nose into that one, but couldn't help wondering what the problem was.

Their friendship blossomed and they would spend days doing things that filled in time and cost nothing. The local library was warm, the internet was free, and you could settle down and read the day's newspapers. On sunny days you could stroll in the gardens around the magnificent Exhibition Building or even walk around Melbourne's CBD.

'I think this is where I'm heading.' Maggie muttered as they passed by a homeless woman camped in the doorway of a Russell Street building. 'I'm already a week behind in my rent.'

Larry was not brave enough to mention Centrelink once again, after Maggies previous reaction to the suggestion. 'I can spare you eighty dollars. That might get that bloody Jackson bloke off your back.'

Larry knew his offer would destroy his budget, but what could he do? Frank Jackson, the rent collector, was a prick and a bully and it was unlikely that a part payment would stop him kicking Maggie out.

'Worse comes to worse you can bunk in my room. I could sleep on the floor. Mind you, we'd have to keep it a secret from Jackson or else he'd put my rent up, then we'd both be in the shit.'

'Thanks Larry. We'll see.' They were friends but such an arrangement would be extending her trust to a whole new level.

Within ten days she had to trust Larry and moved her belongings into his room when Jackson gave her her marching orders. They managed to keep the arrangement a secret from the landlord for weeks. Larry had picked up an inflatable mattress from a camp store and true to his word slept on the floor. On the one occasion Jackson caught Maggie coming out of Larry's room, she spun him a yarn that Larry was paying her to clean his room once a week.

'He's bloody hopeless. Pays me just to sweep his floors and do his washing. I don't suppose you know of anybody else who's needing a cleaner Mr Jackson?' She was hoping he would swallow this bullshit. All those years of practice spinning tales to her husband, to avoid his wrath, had made her an expert.

Jackson gave Maggie a sceptical look with his beady eyes. 'Nope. I can't imagine anyone here could afford to pay. In fact, I'm surprised Larry can pay you. He looks like he couldn't afford a pot to piss in.'

'I don't ask him where he gets his money. Long as he pays.' She headed to the front door. 'See you next week, maybe.'

Maggie scurried down the street hoping the bastard of a landlord had believed her cover story. She realised she and Larry couldn't keep this subterfuge up indefinitely. She looked in shop windows until she caught sight of Jackson's reflection leaving the premises and was then able to return.

CHAPTER SEVEN

'I think we have to give the funerals are rest for a while. The last thing I need is getting my name or picture in the paper and having Brian find me. I swear he will kill me and probably you too.' Maggie was still shaken by the whole CPR incident yesterday.

'Sorry, but we couldn't let the poor bugger die,' said Larry. In reality, he knew he might have held back and hoped somebody else would come to the rescue, if it hadn't been for Henry's presence. 'I agree about giving it a rest. We'll think of some other ways to get by.'

'Here! Give me a hand taking the sheets off and then gather up your dirty clothes. Today we will lash out and visit the laundromat.' Maggie was in one of those moods, not a time to offer alternative plans for the day.

They carried their laundry to a nearby laundromat and spent a precious six dollars in the machines. A couple of moulded plastic chairs provided them with a spot to sit and watch laundry tumble around in the washer. Larry couldn't help but reflect on how his whole life was now a tangled mess tumbling around. He was pleased when it came to drying that somebody had left about eight minutes of drying time on one of the clothes dryers. A small win, but a win.

Maggie eventually broke her stony silence. 'So, tell me about your mate Henry. I assume he was in jail with you. What did he do, eh? Murder his wife?'

'Nah, look I know you don't like him for some reason, but he's not a bad bloke.'

Maggie looked less than convinced, so Larry tried to explain.

'Okay, sure, he killed a bloke. But it wasn't deliberate. He was pissed and had a car accident and his passenger died. He was jailed for culpable driving or whatever they call it. He wouldn't hurt a fly, despite being built like an oversized rugby player.'

Larry gave her a wry smile. 'Everybody was scared of him, because of his nickname *Henry the Hammer* and assumed he had committed some crime with a hammer. Whenever he was asked why he was inside, he just say he killed a bloke, which just fed the rumour. His surname was Hamer, so it's pretty bloody obvious how he got Hammer as a nick name. They're not always the smartest guys inside.'

'Well, you managed to end up there, didn't you?' Maggie sure was in a mood.

'I know it was the stupidest thing I ever did. Look at me now. Poor as buggery living in a squat. The only good thing in my life is you.' He actually really meant it although it sounded just a bit too smooth. It certainly brought a smile to Maggie's face.

'Nice try, sunshine. You think you can talk your way into the good books? You sound almost as sleazy as your mate.'

'We did a few courses together at Golden Hills, including CPR. Henry reckoned it would impress the Parole Board and I think he was probably right. I haven't seen or heard from him since.'

'What was all the Prof nonsense? '

'Pretty funny hey? Just because I could use a computer, they thought I was smart and gave me Prof as a nick name. I sure had 'em fooled.'

Maggie smiled at him for the second time. 'You certainly aren't dumb Larry; you just made some dumb choices in the past. You get sucked in by others too easily. Look at you taking me on board.'

'I think the sheets are dry. You want me to get them out of the dryer.' Larry was keen to change the subject. Together they folded the sheets and put them into their striped bag.

The rest of their clothes were soon dry and packed away in the bag and so they lugged them back home to Heather Street.

After a lunch of jam sandwiches made at home, they made their way through the streets to the Yarra River, that much maligned waterway that snaked its way through Melbourne. A sealed track followed the course of the river shared by pedestrians and many, often speeding, cyclists. It really provided quite a peaceful setting and they enjoyed exploring its possibilities.

Side by side they meandered along the path through the Collingwood Children's Farm, an area of the river flats that had been set up to house farm animals. Being a Saturday, it was crowded with families enjoying farm animals only four kilometres from Melbourne's CBD. They crossed under the Johnston Street bridge and followed the river upstream on the Collingwood side of the Yarra. In many ways the river formed a social divide as Kew was an up-market suburb compared with Collingwood. However, like so many inner-city suburbs across the world, Collingwood was undergoing gentrification.

On the Collingwood side they passed under a number of English Plane trees and other deciduous intruders on the native vegetation. The path was often overshadowed by apartment developments, not so across the river on the Kew side where there was a large area of native vegetation, part of the Yarra Bend Park. As they made their way upstream, the river bubbled over rocks and developed into mild rapids. When they had walked as far as Dight's Falls, they sat on a bench and watched the river tumble over a weir about a metre in height. Hardly a waterfall. Birds abounded and a pair of Kookaburras cast suspicious eyes in their direction from a huge eucalypt nearby.

'This must have been upgraded, I am sure it has been replaced. I remember as a kid once having a picnic around here,' said Larry airing his local knowledge to the Sydneysider. 'It was originally built way back when Melbourne was brand new to provide water for a flour mill.'

'You never really told me much about your life as a kid,' Maggie replied.

'Melbourne was certainly different then. My dad was a carpenter and he built our house about five kilometres east of here at North Balwyn. It was on the outer edge of Melbourne, a mixture of new houses and paddocks when I was a youngster. Me and me brother used to have a great time mucking around down in a nearby creek, building cubbies and playing all sorts of games. Now it's an uppity suburb, almost considered inner city. '

'What about your brother? '

'He was older than me. Got drafted into the army when his birthdate was pulled out in the lottery they used back then. They had to expand the army to keep sending troops to Vietnam. He went over there for about twelve months and was never the same.' Larry paused for a moment before he continued. 'When he came back, he couldn't settle. He roamed Australia trying his hand at all sorts of jobs. Eventually he ended up on a prawn boat out of Carnarvon in WA. He fell overboard one night and was never found. At least that was the official line. I reckon he just decided he'd had enough.'

Maggie reached out and squeezed Larry's hand. He continued 'Dad never got over it and died of a heart attack two years later. Mum followed with cancer the following year.'

The sound of the water tumbling over the falls provided the background for a moment or two of reflection.

'What about your childhood Maggie?'

'Let's leave that till another day. Come on we'd better walk back before it rains.'

Clouds were building up in the west and they retraced their steps. They made it home just in time to check on the position of the old bucket and the paint tin in the hall.

Later that night Maggie woke from a disturbing dream. She struggled to return to sleep and lay awake thinking back over her life.

Her mother Laura had given birth to her as a teenager and had been unprepared to put her life on hold, leaving much of Maggie's care to her mother, Glenys. Soon after Maggie's third birthday Laura up and left for a trip to Europe leaving Maggie with her grandmother. She would not return for ten years.

Glenys had raised Maggie as if she were her own child and most people in fact assumed she was just a mature mother. Maggie called her Ma which did nothing to change people's assumptions. When Laura did eventually return from London for a brief visit, she showed limited interest in her daughter. Maggie remembered as a thirteen-year-old being crushed by her mother's indifference. She withdrew into herself and became somewhat of an isolate.

Maggie realised now how vulnerable she had been in her late twenties when she met Brian through work. He had swept her off her feet. Somebody other than Ma actually cared for her.

If only she made different choices. After high school, she spent eighteen months as a McDonalds team member and then was lucky enough to be employed in a suburban real-estate office as a receptionist. What if she had been able to afford to go to university? What if she had been content to work up to store manager at Maccas? How different would her life had been if she had never met Brian? What ifs? Maybes? A bit like that movie *Sliding Doors*

CHAPTER EIGHT

Jimmy was still trying to get his head around all that had happened. Here he was lying in a hospital bed hooked up to a machine that seemed it was monitoring a whole lot of his vital functions. He could remember being at Richard Nelson's funeral and according to the nurses he had suffered a heart attack. Vague memories were returning of the ambulance siren as they rushed him to the Alfred hospital where a team of medical workers were waiting for him. They all pounced on him to hook him up to various bits of equipment; calmly issuing instructions to each other. In just a few minutes he was in an operating theatre being asked about his pain.

'On a scale of one to ten, how does it feel?' the masked woman had asked him.

'Eight. It's not as bad as in the ambulance,' he had managed to reply.

'Of course it's a bit better, the oxygen helps. Wait till we have those stents in and you'll feel as good as new."

Well, that wasn't quite right, was it? He still felt like shit.

The chest pain may have disappeared, but the tenderness and bruising around his groin was unbelievable. Bruising, a shade of purple, extended from just below his navel to halfway down his right thigh. And boy was it tender down there. Apparently, they had fed all their repairing gear up through a vein in his groin. It was mind boggling stuff, as far as Jimmy was concerned.

He had to stay lying on his back for a day or so and was pissing into a bottle. When it was all boiled down, he decided he didn't have too much to complain about, he was still alive. Gee, his heart attack could have happened somewhere else where there weren't clever people about to save him. Imagine if it happened in his secret love nest in Hawthorn when he was with Gemma or Nicole; they would have been no use. He must find out who did the CPR on him at Dick's funeral and thank them.

As he lay there, his thoughts went back to the afternoon before the funeral. He had taken the afternoon off as there were no races being run. Nicole had met him at the flat he secretly kept in Hawthorn. Well, his wife Sophie knew he owned a block of flats in Hawthorn. What she didn't know was that he kept one for his own private use for the occasional dalliance with a couple of his special friends. There had been a time in his life, when as a bookmaker he had been awash with money, hence the block of flats. Now that on-line gambling had taken off and was dominated by international betting companies, he had started living a more modest lifestyle. Still, he and Nicole had spent a pleasant afternoon and he blamed the sparkling wine for his indigestion that put an end to their more active love making. Perhaps that had been a warning. Still the pleasant thoughts remained as he drifted off to sleep.

'Are you up for a visitor Mr O'Connor?' asked the nurse before she realised Jimmy was dozing.

'Is it the wife again?' he opened his eyes. Sophie had been in already once today.

'Nope. It's another lady. Umm. She said she was an Izzy Nelson, Richard's daughter.'

'Oh! Okay I will see her. Thanks Bianca.' He had read the nurse's name tag and made a point of using her name. A book he had read years ago stressed how using people's names made them feel better towards you.

Within minutes a woman, about mid-thirties, put her head around the door.

'Is it alright if I pop in for a minute or two.' She was an attractive full-figured woman with dark brown eyes, not the sort Jimmy would ever turn away.

'Sure, come in I could do with a pretty face to cheer me up.'

'Hi Mr O'Connor.'

'Oh, call me Jimmy for God's sake!' Did he really look that old?

'Okay Jimmy. I'm Izzy, Richard Nelson's third daughter. We were all so upset when you collapsed at the funeral. My sisters and I just wanted to check that you were doing okay.'

'Yeah, thanks Izzy. They reckon I will be as good as new in a few months if I take it easy. It's bloody amazing what they can do these days. Isn't it?'

'Yes, it is,' she agreed.

'Look I am so sorry. I must apologise for upsetting the whole funeral. I was so lucky that somebody knew what to do. Eh?'

'It was two men actually. One was Henry Hamer, but we can't work out who the other fellow was. He must have been another of Dad's racing mates. We looked in the condolence book, but that was no use. Of course, not everybody signed it I guess.'

'Gee Izzy I would really like to thank these heroes. Any chance you could get this Henry bloke to give me a visit?'

'I can check through Dad's mobile and see if he's listed.' She gave him a smile that reminded him of Gemma. Probably not the best for his repaired heart. 'Listen Jimmy don't you worry about messing up the funeral. Personally, I was glad there was the distraction. It made talking to all those people, I don't really know, so much easier.'

'Happy to be a distraction, but look I was really sorry about Dick's, I mean your dad's passing.'

'Thanks. It wasn't a big shock he had been only given a couple of months. I'll get onto tracking down Henry for you. You take care now." She gave him another of those smiles and she left.

Henry pushed open the door of 35E hoping he had the right room. The patient in the bed was Jimmy O'Connor; he had the image of the man burnt into his brain somewhere along with the whole funeral experience. He didn't look much better than when he was carted off in the ambulance and was still hooked up to some monitoring device. His head turned from staring out the window towards Henry and he looked puzzled for just a moment or two and then he managed a smile.

'I bet you're Henry. Am I right?'

'Yes Jimmy, glad to meet you again. Izzy said you wanted to see me.'

Jimmy nodded toward the chair. 'Come in. Sit down. I gather I owe you and the other bloke my life?'

Henry sat facing the bed. 'I think that might be laying it on a bit thick. If we hadn't done CPR then I'm sure somebody else would have had a crack.'

'So, where's your mate? I need to thank him also.'

'Larry is a bit of a shy type. He's having a few issues at the moment. Going through a bit of a rough patch from what I can gather. I doubt he's got two bob to rub together.'

'Perhaps I can help him out? I'm not without a few connections and such. God, I'm not going to be doing much for a while. Basically, I'm fucked. Well, a little bit fucked for a while. Tell me about your mate's woes. It might distract me from my own.'

So, Henry told him what little he could about Larry,

explaining that he and his partner must be having trouble finding suitable accommodation without giving too many details about how they had met. Jimmy listened and once again his face lit up with a smile.

'Serendipity mate. It's serendipity. I think I can help him out while at the same time he will be helping me out. I'd better explain. See I've this block of flats in Hawthorn that are all rented out except one which I keep for my own use, if you know what I mean.'

Henry looked puzzled. 'You live in the flat?'

'Oh no. Only a couple of afternoons each week with a couple of special friends that Sophie, the wife doesn't know about. Now I won't be using it for months by the look of things. They could move in and keep an eye on things for me. How does that sound?'

'Sounds good to me, really generous of you. I'll ask them.'

'Now you my friend, I wonder if you could contact those girls of mine and explain my misfortune. I am sure they will need consoling.' Jimmy attempted to laugh at his own joke but could feel it pull at his heart strings. His heart was in no shape to have its strings pulled.

'I really think you should contact them yourself,' replied Henry, not wanting to be involved in Jimmy's love life and be the bearer of bad news.

Jimmy put on his anxious look. 'The doc said I wasn't to do anything stressful.'

'Okay, I'll see what I can do. You better give me the details about this flat.'

For the next ten minutes they discussed all the particulars and Henry jotted down the important parts on the back of a get-well card which was sitting on the bedside cupboard. By this stage Jimmy was ready for a bit more shut eye and bid his saviour goodbye.

CHAPTER NINE

Melbourne had lived up to its reputation for the last four days. It is renowned for having the weather typical of four seasons in one day. But it was almost springtime and everything seemed to be alive. Maggie couldn't help but feel optimistic. Her distress over the drama at the Brighton funeral was fading. On reflection she had seen a new side of Larry, doing something few people could manage. She had always thought of him as a sweet man and he had gone out of his way to look after her at considerable expense and personal suffering.

He had his head in a book in their bedroom while she was tidying up the kitchen. She wiped down the stainless-steel sink and the small Laminex bench over the cupboards. A worn broom, scrounged from somebody's hard garbage, was all she had to sweep the floor of the dust which blew in and the few mice droppings. It was so good that one cupboard had proved to be mouse proof.

Her mind drifted back to her kitchen in Sydney where

Brian expected her to spend the best part of each day. It is a small wonder he hadn't chained her to the sink. After they were married, he had insisted she leave the job she loved as a receptionist in a real estate office to be a housewife. She did not object at the time as she was hoping to start a family. For whatever reason that didn't happen. Her doctor and the specialist to whom she was referred could find no reason why she couldn't conceive. Brian was not about to have his fertility questioned. He became more controlling. Without her own income he had her close her bank account and she was reliant on him for money to fund the running of the house. She did manage to get a credit card attached to Brian's account but had to justify each purchase.

Someone knocking at the back door snapped her from her daydreaming and she panicked rushing to get Larry to deal with whoever was there. She stayed in the bedroom, sitting on the mattress on the floor and could not quite decipher the conversation that was taking place until Larry called out.

'It's alright Maggie, it's just Henry.'

Henry, that bozo mate of Larry's from the funeral, how did he find them? She went out to the kitchen to join the men.

'Hi there little lady.' Henry gave her that wink again. He hadn't changed in the last five days. 'Surprised to see me?'

'How did you know we were here? You dropped us off up the other end of the street?' her voice clearly showing her anxiety.

'Well, when I dropped you off, I gave Prof my number but then realized in my then inebriated state that I should have got his number. So, I drove around the block and bugger me dead I see you guys sneaking down the lane to this place. You can't bullshit a bullshitter my dear. Why didn't you guys tell me things weren't so rosy?'

Larry was leaning against the sink also stunned by their circumstances being exposed. 'We're getting by mate. Guess we're a bit embarrassed about all this,' Larry waved his arms to indicate the hovel in which they were living, 'and our presence at the funeral was a bit dodgy.'

Henry just laughed. 'Hey, I have a bit to tell you about that. Come on I will shout you lunch at a pub and fill you in.'

'What do you reckon Maggie? Sounds good?' Larry pleaded.

'I'll have to change.' There was no way Maggie was going out to lunch in her worn tracksuit. 'You two can go if you like.'

'Go change if you want. The Prof and I are too ugly to go out without you to even up the score.' The cheesy comments rolled off Henry's tongue so naturally.

They settled around a table set for four in the Bakers Arms. Henry had bought Maggie a glass of white wine and the men each a pot of Carlton Draught. After examining the menu Maggie decided on a warm chicken salad and the blokes chose to have a Chicken Parma, a dish on every pub's menu. Henry went up to the bar to order the food.

'What do you think he wants?' Maggie whispered in Henry's absence.

'Wait and see. Perhaps he just wants to help. People sometimes do that,' he hissed back. Maggie was sometimes just too distrustful.

Henry returned stuffing a bulging wallet into his back pocket. 'I have to tell you what happened after Friday's funeral. You know Izzie, Richard's youngest daughter? She got in touch with me because that bookie we saved from St Peter wanted to see and thank his saviours. His name is Jimmy O'Connor and he was recovering in the Alfred hospital.' He paused for a moment to take a swig of his beer. 'Now I hope you don't mind but I went and saw him myself. I had the impression that young Maggie here wasn't real happy about the whole affair.' He gave Maggie another of those winks and continued on.

'Turns out he is going to be in the care of his wife Sophie for the next few months and is going to be attending some sort of re-hab. He was banging on about rewarding us. I told him that it wasn't necessary for me but I did say I suspected you were doing it tough and finding it hard to get good accommodation.'

Henry took another generous slug of his beer. 'It so happens that our Mr O'Connor has bit of a problem being locked up for a couple of months. He happens to have been keeping secrets from his missus and has a flat across the river in Hawthorn for his own private use. Actually, he owns a whole block of flats but keeps one for entertaining friends.'

Maggie took a sip of her wine half expecting one of those winks if she understood Henry correctly. The wink didn't eventuate as he continued.

'It was his suggestion that you could move into the flat while you try to find accommodation. He doesn't want it left empty and said it would be good to have someone in the block of flats keeping an eye on things. You know. Making sure all the bins get put out, watering the little bit of garden, that sort of thing. What do you reckon? Eh?' He smiled, looking pretty pleased with himself. 'Jimmy said that could be his way of saying thank you.'

'What do think Maggie?' Larry looked at her waiting for her verdict.

'Are you sure there isn't a catch Henry? It's all legit? My name doesn't have to go on any agreement or anything?' Maggie was sceptical as always and was obviously nervous about the deal.

'Who're you hiding from love?' Henry asked.

'Her ex, who's a bash artist,' blurted out Larry who earned himself a kick under the table.

'No names, no pack drill. All you have to do is look after the place until Jimmy is back on his feet.' Henry finished his beer and in a lowered voice said, 'If your ex gives you any trouble you just let me know.'

Maggie imagined the match up. At well over six foot and as solid as he was, Henry would be an even match for Brian and being a few years younger would help. 'It's okay. He's probably still in Sydney and shouldn't have any idea where I am.'

'Here's our lunch now. I'll get some more drinks and you guys have a think about it' Henry returned to the bar as a young Asian woman hovered by their table balancing the three plates on her arms.

'Two Parma's, warm chicken salad?' she said.

'Chicken salad here, thanks,' Maggie directed.

'Awesome. Enjoy,' she replied and dropped the meals in front of them and left.

'We don't have much to lose, do we? But it does sound pretty strange. Don't you agree?' She raised her eyebrows waiting for Larry to reply.

'A couple of months will be great. I may be able to find some work if we have a proper place to live, with a bit of luck,' said Larry.

'I will try too, I've shown I'm a pretty good dish pig. Who knows what else I can do?' Maggie looked up to see Henry returning with their drinks.

They all settled into eating. It was quite some time since Maggie and Larry had sat down and eaten a regular meal. Henry laughed as Maggie reached across and stole a chip off Larry's plate and shook his index finger in her direction. 'No thieves allowed at this table.' It took Maggie a second or two to get the joke before she joined in with a giggle.

After they had all finished eating and had a third drink it was agreed they should make the most of Jimmy's offer. Another two rounds of drinks and the consensus was that it would be rude not to accept his proposal.

CHAPTER TEN

Maggie was sitting in the back seat with one of their striped bags beside her. Henry turned left out of Riversdale Road into Butterfly Court. It was no more than two hundred metres long, lined with paperbark trees. The block of cream brick flats was almost at the far end. It looked as if it was built in about the 1960's with a few shrubs growing between it and the footpath. A driveway went up one side leading to a row of carports with numbers painted on the concrete paving.

Henry pulled the BMW into a vacant carport. 'Let's see if we can get you settled.' He went to the far post of the carport where at the bottom of the post was attached a lock box. 'Jimmy said the code was 3122, Hawthorn's postcode. Not the most secure choice, in my opinion.'

He punched in the numbers, opened the box and triumphantly held up a set of keys. 'Follow me,' he said as he led the way into the nearest stairwell. 'Apparently number ten is here at the back on the second level.'

Maggie was impressed with the state of the stairwell.

The entrance was tiled with a potted Monstera in a corner and the stairs were carpeted. Up on the second level was their new home. The flat had a small entrance hall with a kitchen off to the right. She couldn't help but feel a little bit disappointed as it looked like a kitchen from the 1960s. Narrow laminex benchtops, a white tiled splashback behind the narrow kitchen sink. A gas hot water heater hung on the wall above the sink. She could only guess that cooking wasn't high on this Jimmy bloke's priorities.

'Wow! This is lovely,' she cried as she looked in the next doorway. The bathroom had been modernised and included a walk-in shower with modern vanity and close-coupled toilet. A combined washing machine and dryer sat in one corner. Jimmy had obviously spent up big on the bathroom. Maggie knew about bathroom renovations as her Sydney home had undergone one. She remembered the belting she had received because Brian thought she was being too friendly with the plumber.

The two men were in the room on the other side of the hallway having a laugh about something. When she looked into what was a bedroom it made her cringe. The walls were painted a deep crimson and large mirror doors on the built-in robe provided a reflected view of the bed made up with satin linen. Bedside tables were adorned with large candles. A large flat screen television was mounted on the wall at the foot of the bed. What on earth did this man get up to in this apartment?

'What do you reckon Maggie? Really tasteful?' said Henry adding one of his signature winks.

'Let's see the rest,' she replied ignoring his tease. The second bedroom was a disappointment as it was filled with packed cardboard boxes apart from a desktop computer sitting on a table in one corner. This was not to provide an alternative to Jimmy's love nest.

A living room nicely furnished with a gas fireplace and another flat screen television was the last room to explore. Henry crossed the room to the fireplace and picked up a mobile phone off the mantle.

'This is Jimmy's spare mobile phone. I just need to get a couple of numbers off it and then the Prof and I will go down and bring up your stuff. Jimmy said if you have any problems, you can call him using this phone. His number is in his contacts as James.'

Maggie wandered from room to room as the two men went downstairs to retrieve their meagre belongings. She was relieved to find towels and a set of cotton sheets in the hall's linen cupboard and set to work stripping the satin sheets from the bed and remaking it with the crisp white cotton set. Further exploration found the refrigerator held nothing but sparkling white wine and Victorian Bitter beer. The freezer section was empty except for a number of ice packs. She realized their luck had changed. Having use of a flat was wonderful but she couldn't help the way she felt. The place gave her the creeps.

Larry and Henry came in the front door both a bit short of breath from the climb up the stairs carrying those bags of possessions.

'I'd better get out to Cranbourne and do some work. There's a race meeting coming up next Wednesday. I'll leave you two to get settled in,' said Henry wiping the sweat from his forehead with his sleeve. One more wink and he was gone.

Later after they had unpacked their belongings and stored them away, they left the flat to explore the area. They walked up Riversdale Road and found a few shops at the corner of Glenferrie Road; a grocery store and an op shop among them. Maggie took little interest in the smart cafés and restaurants which were not going to suit their budget. The grocery store provided some essentials and they headed back to their new abode. Despite her misgivings about the nature of the Hawthorn flat she suddenly felt more secure than she had for a long time.

'Here, give me one of the bags Larry; you don't have to treat me like a queen all the time,' she giggled.

'We should've taken a chariot,' was Larry's reply as a tram rattled down the hill passed them.

'No need. Let's just enjoy our new neighbourhood,' said Maggie as her eyes took in the few old stately homes yet to fall victim to developers, keen to build apartment blocks.

'You know I am sorry I was mad at you about the whole Brighton funeral drama. It's because of that we now have a true roof over our heads, even if it's a bit creepy.'

The unease Maggie felt dissipated over the next few weeks and they commenced to live a relatively normal, but very frugal existence. They enjoyed walks in the local parks and along the tree-lined streets of Hawthorn. Often, they admired some of the older, imposing homes that were found mixed in among modern architect-designed dwellings where the wrecking ball had cleared a site. The opportunity shop near the corner of Glenferrie Road received a number of visits and Maggie tried on a number of stylish dresses and settled on a blue and black side panel dress by *Jaqui El* for $8. She had never before had a designer labelled frock.

Larry tried to fulfil Jimmy's request about looking after the block of flats. He made sure the bins were wheeled to the curb on a Monday night and brought back in on Tuesday morning. Some of the tenants were pretty lazy and left rubbish, particularly cardboard boxes, beside the bins. Why they could not crush them or tear them sufficiently to fit in the recycle bins was a mystery. Larry didn't really mind as sorting out such problems gave him a sense of purpose. Although he would soon be eligible for the age pension he started to consider trying once again to get a job. It would be just a little bit easier now they had a fixed address.

CHAPTER ELEVEN

Maggie could not believe how good she felt about the world. She walked along the path beside the Yarra River in Fairview Park. Activity on the river caught her attention and she paused to watch. A rowing boat with eight teenage girls dressed in matching maroon tops was moving up stream. Their oars sliced through the water with a coordinated rhythm thanks to a small girl sitting at the front barking at her crew. Oh, to be young again!

The park was busy with dog owners letting their animals run, chase and fetch on the large open space. She resumed her stroll along with the other walkers and joggers who pounded the pathways. People were so friendly and those not plugged into some listening device said good morning or at least gave a smile or nod. She smiled to herself as she thought over what had happened in the early hours of the morning.

She had been half awake and had been immersed in the comfort of Larry's arms. He loved to spoon and she could tell by his breathing that he was asleep. But that was not a gun in his pocket pressing into her back. Was he dreaming of her or someone else? She had pondered this in her drowsy condition. Could she really be jealous of the person in his dreams? That was ridiculous. Despite loving Larry, all the time she had been with him she had said no to his advances. It was not like Larry was anything like her bastard of a husband who was responsible for putting her off sex for so long. In her drowsy spell she listened to Larry murmuring in his sleep.

She giggled to herself as she decided it was time they consummated their partnership. After she made her intentions clear, Larry was quick to ask her if she was sure of her decision.

What was to follow was something she would never forget. He smothered her with kisses and caresses. Never had anyone treated her like this before; for her, this was a completely new experience. The feel of Larry's lips was still with her. Her ex-husband had never behaved in such a way, never concerned with her pleasure. She couldn't remember ever having enjoyed sex so much and could only hope they had not disturbed the neighbours. When morning filtered its way through the blinds she was still entwined in his arms and was the happiest she had been in years.

When she reached the end of the park, she followed the path around a playing field and headed home. She couldn't help noticing the exercise gear worn by the other walkers and joggers. All flash active wear with brand names like

Lorna Jane or recognisable trademarks like the Nike tick clearly displayed. What a contrast to her second-hand Kmart fleecy tracksuit. But today she couldn't care less.

Larry sat at the computer in the spare room. He was trying to put together his resume while Maggie was out walking. How could he explain the gap of over four years in his work history? He had no formal qualifications in bookkeeping other than his over thirty years' experience keeping the books for Appleton's. He had kept up to date with technology and had mastered a number of accounting software packages. Unfortunately, nobody was going to give him a reference given the embezzlement he had been sucked into. There were a few simple bookkeeping jobs advertised online at which he could easily be successful. A police check seemed so common these days, a hurdle too high to get over for any job with responsibility. Perhaps he should not aim so high and just look for another shit job, similar to his last in a warehouse, as a storeman.

He sat there staring at the screen lost in thought. His thoughts soon wandered to the change in Maggie. Out of the blue she had finally consented to sex. He was somewhat embarrassed, after all he was seriously out of practice. He had really tried to be gentle with Maggie. His ex-wife, Jennifer, had always been critical of his needs and had made sure he cared for hers. Perhaps after all, he should be thankful for

Jennifer's bossy nature and detailed instructions. He was so glad Maggie seemed so cheery with him this morning. If he could just nail down a job, he could provide her with a normal life. He really loved her and wished he could erase her troubled past or at least offer her a future.

CHAPTER TWELVE

'You just have to try a bit harder Lee. That front page spread in the *Daily Telegraph* has got everybody wound up. Talk back radio callers are making us out as stupid.'

Senior Constable Danny Lee looked up from his computer screen at his boss and shook his head. 'The resolution on all the dash cam footage and CCTV from the house across the road is pretty ordinary. I'll keep looking. We will get there Sir.'

Another road rage incident had the press really stirred up this time. It seems the victim, a Jake Cummins, driving a Subaru Forester had upset the guy driving the Nissan Patrol on the Pacific Highway at Roseville. Mr Cummins had been followed home by the Nissan Patrol. Danny had done well to collect the images from the neighbour's CCTV and dash cam footage people had provided via *Crime Stoppers*. Unfortunately, the media seemed to have better pictures.

Ten minutes later, things were looking up.

'Sir, I think this one's better. You can see the guy from

the Nissan punch our Mr Cummins and then he gets a jack handle out of his boot and smashes every window of the Subaru.' Danny paused the video. 'I just can't quite make out the rego plate. The first part looks like it's either AJ1 or it might be AJ7. That should be enough.'

Sure enough, in a few minutes, a search of all New South Wales registration plates produced only five Nissan Patrols with those first combinations. Three of those were outside Sydney, in regional districts, so pretty unlikely. There was one based in Parramatta and one in Chatswood.

'I'd bet all your chopsticks on the Chatswood one, young Danny.'

The Senior Constable ignored the racist quip from his sergeant. It was his grandfather who had made his way to Australia from China just before the communist took over in 1949. Danny had put up with crap like that all his life and knew where he would like to shove some chopsticks.

'I think you're right Sir. It's registered to one Brian John Bennington.'

'You're not Wong, Lee.' The sergeant thought himself hilarious. 'Take Constable MacDonald with you and go and have a chat with Mr Bennington.'

Danny parked the car outside Bennington's address and looked up at the house high up above street level. Sure enough there was an aging Nissan Patrol with the plate

AJ 12 FB parked in a carport down at the base of the steep block.

'Records show his wife had to have an AVO issued on him a while back, after a domestic violence report. Now Jess, we just have to be a bit careful with this guy. If he is our guy, he may have a very short fuse.'

Constable Jess MacDonald took one look at the steps leading up to the house and said, 'I'd be a bit cranky if I had to climb these stairs every time I came home.'

'Come on, it will be good exercise,' said Danny taking the steps two at a time in an attempt to impress the pretty young constable. By the time he reached the front door he was regretting his macho display. What was worse was that Jess was just behind him and not short of breath. He pressed the button for the doorbell. They exchanged looks as they listened for activity inside the house. Footsteps grew louder before the large four panel door opened.

At tall man looking remarkably like the pixelated image from the CCTV stood before them. His face matched the drivers licence photo despite missing a moustache.

'Huh, what do you want?'

'We are looking for Mr Brian John Bennington; I assume that's you Sir.'

'Yep, that's me, so what?'

'We'd like to ask you a few questions. Could we come inside?' Danny made every effort to be civil.

'Can't you just say what you want?'

'We would like to know where you were on Friday at 4.30 in the afternoon, Mr Bennington.'

'Minding my own bloody business,' was the smart-arse reply.

'In that case Mr Bennington I am placing you under arrest for assault and malicious damage to private property.' Danny had had enough. 'Tell him Constable.'

Jess rattled off the standard warning about his rights. Brian looked as if he was about to explode but managed to restrict his rage to an outburst.

'Think ya so fucking smart. You'll keep, you silly bitch. You too, you slanty eyed prick.'

Danny putting on an exaggerated Aussie accent said 'Enough of the insults thanks Cobber. Put your hands out in front please.'

Despite his face turning beet red, Bennington cooperated with the handcuffs. On Danny's suggestion, they all entered the house to retrieve the house keys from the kitchen bench so the hilltop home could be locked.

They took care descending the steps down to the road ignoring the mutterings of Mr Bennington and their urges to give him a decent shove.

CHAPTER THIRTEEN

Larry dropped the plate back in the sink and raced towards the scream. Maggie was hunched on the couch all the colour having drained from her face.

'What's wrong? Are you in pain?' Larry crouched beside the couch reaching out to Maggie placing his hands on her shoulders as she trembled violently and pulled away into a foetal position.

Between her sobs she eventually pointed at the television and said, 'It's him.'

Larry looked at the television as a detective was interviewed about a victim of a road rage incident. He sat beside her on the couch and held her in his arms as the news program broke for a commercial.

'You tell me what this is about when you're ready Dear.' Larry tried to be patient. Maggie was terrified by something she had seen on the news. Was this what they called a panic attack?

'It's all right. Deep breaths,' he murmured, having heard

characters go on about breathing and deep breaths on television dramas.

After three or four minutes of Larry's cooing and stroking Maggie was able to explain. 'It was Brian, my ex, bashing up some poor bloke in his driveway.'

'Where?'

'In the bloke's driveway.'

'No, no, I mean where? As in here? In Melbourne?' asked Larry.

'I think it was Sydney. It's national news. The police want to catch him, they said.'

'If it's in Sydney you have nothing to worry about. In fact, you could telephone them and dob him in.'

The minute he had made the suggestion he knew it was a mistake. Maggie once again became distressed and sobbed. 'No way. What if he found me? He would kill us both.'

'Sorry dumb idea. How about I make us a cuppa?' This was another idea straight off a television drama. Larry was glad he had watched a lot of television during those three years at Golden Hills. He retreated to the kitchen and popped a couple of tea bags in mugs and dumped a paper sachet of sugar into one of the mugs as the kettle boiled. Those sugar packets were so often left behind on the outside tables of cafes, probably to be thrown away when the dirty coffee cups were cleared. He returned to the living room with the hot tea.

'Wow, how much sugar did you put in the tea?' she actually

almost smiled. 'You think I need it. Thanks sunshine.'

'I don't think you should worry. The cops will work out who he is. They might even lock him up.' he reassured. 'Some poor bugger might have to share a cell with him,' Larry mused.

'I'm sure they'll catch up with Mr Claymore, so you shouldn't worry,' Larry said trying to sound reassuring.

'His name is Bennington, Brian Bennington not Claymore. I have been using my maiden name here in Melbourne.' Once again, she almost smiled. 'I suppose I'm probably still married to him, even though I call him my ex.'

'Maggie Claymore sounds pretty good to me. Try to forget him, you've found a suitable replacement.' Larry rarely sang his own praises but being better than a thug was hardly bragging.

That night Maggie battled to get to sleep and when she did manage to drift off her dreams took her back to Sydney and her fear of a thumping. She dreamt of trying to keep the silliest secrets from Brian who seemed to disapprove of anything she did, especially outside the home. How could he not trust her to be part of a book club? He accused her of having an affair on more than one occasion when he had telephoned home and she had happened to be out.

There was no point in arguing as it would lead to her being thrown against a wall, or some suffering some similar mistreatment. Why did she stay with him all those years? This was a question she could not answer.

The following morning their Weet-Bix was interrupted by Jimmy's mobile phone playing Greensleeves. Larry picked it up and poked at the accept icon on the screen.

'Hello. Names Larry, who's calling?'

'It's me Prof. Who was you expecting? The tax office?' Henry chuckled at his own joke. 'I was ringing to see if you and the lovely little lady would like to go out to lunch today. My shout.'

'I'd just better check with Maggie.'

'Smart move mate. Tell her it's just at a pub so she doesn't have to get too glammed up. I want you to meet a friend of mine.'

Larry put the phone down and asked Maggie if she was happy to accept Henry's invitation. She gave a nodded approval, for although Henry annoyed her at times, they were not in a position to turn down a free feed. Back on the phone, Henry told them he would pick them up around twelve.

CHAPTER FOURTEEN

She pondered the clothes in her wardrobe. It was difficult to decide what to wear. Nicoletta Donnelly hadn't hesitated in accepting another invitation to lunch with Henry as she had felt at a loss on Thursdays, since Jimmy's heart attack. Eventually she settled on a pair of camel coloured capri pants with a dark brown cowl necked top. Her favourite crimson sweater with a vee neck showed just a bit too much cleavage. She wanted to look her best; but knowing that Henry knew of her relationship with Jimmy, she went for a conservative appearance. She didn't want him or his friends to view her as Jimmy's doxy.

Being a single mother had been a real challenge. Hairdressers don't make a fortune unless they have their own salon and there were always bills to pay. Nicole, only her aging mother still called her Nicoletta, had little time or opportunity to do things for herself. A neighbour was very kind in looking after Anthony after school and on Saturday mornings. Working Saturdays meant she had Thursdays off work and was able to catch up on shopping, errands needing attention and visiting her mother in residential aged care. That was until Jimmy entered her life.

Three years ago, her father-in-law had passed away and despite having little contact with him since Patrick's death she went to his funeral mass. It was at the wake that she had met Jimmy who was a second cousin to her late husband Patrick. He had offered to take her and nine-year-old Anthony to a country race meeting and get up close to the horses, behind the scenes. Anthony had *the best day ever* and it wasn't just because he missed a Thursday of school. Nicole agreed to meet Jimmy the following Thursday for lunch.

For the last three years she had spent time on most Thursdays with Jimmy, more often than not in his secret flat in Hawthorn. He had been kind and generous to her and what's more she enjoyed the physical aspects of being his *special friend*, although she suspected at times that she may not have been his only one. She much preferred this arrangement compared to how some of the other women in the salon were swiping right or left on their dating apps.

When she had received a phone call from Henry filling her in on Jimmy's health issues she had dissolved into tears on the phone. The poor man was at a loss not knowing what to do, but to his credit he rang back the following day to check on her wellbeing. He told her the whole story of Jimmy's collapse at the funeral and he had talked her into meeting him for coffee on Thursday. The irony of funerals being so significant in her relationships was not lost on Nicole. A week later, once again on a Thursday, they had met for lunch, and she enjoyed his company.

Today he had once again asked her to lunch but fore-warned her he wanted to bring along a couple for her to meet. Apparently, the bloke had helped Henry bring Jimmy back from the Pearly Gates. Initially she was a little disap-pointed that he wasn't going to pick her up and she had to find her own way to the pub he had chosen. Then again, she was not in a big rush to advance their friendship.

Her ancient Corolla coughed and spluttered down the drive of her North Blackburn home before it fired on all four cylin-ders. She nursed it towards the city, to the pub in Auburn. It was easy to find a parking spot up a side street and she recognised Henry's BMW parked nearby. A final check of her appearance in the cars mirror before she nervously made her way to the pub's Bistro entrance, glad she was not the first to arrive.

CHAPTER FIFTEEN

At just a few minutes after twelve the old BMW pulled up in the driveway and Larry and Maggie went down to meet Henry. The blinds on unit number eight parted as Mrs Gentry kept tabs on what was going on.

'Oh my. Don't you look a bit of all right?' Henry exclaimed when he saw Maggie. 'I told Larry you didn't have to get glammed up. That shade of blue matches your eyes.' This was followed by his trademark wink.

For once Maggie was not offended by Henry's comment for she did feel pleased with her appearance. The eight-dollar panelled dress she had bought from the op shop was a perfect fit. She loved the cobalt blue and the black side panels created a flattering shape to her slim figure.

'It's just a dress, you silly man!' said Maggie with a giggle as she climbed into the back seat. 'But thanks for the compliment.'

They drove up Riversdale Road to a hotel near Auburn Road, parking in a side street with a two-hour parking limit.

The bistro had only a few patrons and they seated themselves at a table for four. Henry went to the bar to buy drinks.

'I feel bad with Henry paying for everything,' Maggie whispered to Larry.

'He was pretty insistent,' replied Harry. 'I wonder who he wants us to meet.'

Henry returned with two beers and a bottle of white wine with two glasses. *A bit of a clue there* thought Maggie. He filled a glass for her.

'Cheers.' He raised his glass. 'Is it okay if we hold off ordering lunch until my friend Nicole gets here?' Maggie nearly choked on her wine. Nicole was one of the contacts in Jimmy's phone; she was guessing it was one and the same. Henry noticed Maggie's reaction and thought an explanation was in order; although he was somewhat amused that Larry was oblivious to what was going on.

'Yeah, you guessed didn't you sweetie? Nicole is one of Jimmy's girlfriends that I was asked to inform that he would be indisposed for a while. We sort of just hit it off. She's a good sport and hasn't had an easy life.'

He had no sooner said this than a woman came through the door, giving him a huge smile as she walked towards their table. She looked about forty years old with possibly a mediterranean background. Her dark hair was in a long bob style and she was full figured. Henry rose to his feet and his new friend stood on tip toes and kissed him on both cheeks.

'Nicole this is Maggie and Larry although I call him Prof,

cos he's sort of smart with computers,' said Henry. They chatted about the weather and other fairly trivial topics. Nicole let on that she was in fact a hairdresser and she had a teenage son. There was little Maggie and Larry were prepared to divulge to a stranger.

They studied the lunch menu displayed on the large blackboard before Larry and Henry went up to the bar to order the meals and pick up some more drinks.

'So how have things been going at the flat, mate?' Henry enquired.

'Great. I can't thank you enough for arranging it all. Maggie loves it although she had an upset yesterday. Chucked a real wobbly.'

'What was the problem? You wash the coloured clothes with the whites?' Henry chuckled.

'No, she saw her dickhead of a husband on some news footage undergoing rage road or whatever it's called. It brought back all her memories of the hidings he gave her. He's up in Sydney, so she shouldn't worry about the prick. The cops are trying to identify him.'

'If he gives her any trouble you let me know Prof. I know a few blokes in Sydney that could have a chat with him; if you know what I mean. Any rate, the cops should track him down and deal with him: tell her to forget the bastard. Here, you cart this bottle of wine back to the girls and I'll bring the beers in a sec.'

Back at the table the women were talking in hushed

tones before the men settled back at the table.

'Hey Henry, what's with the bottle of wine we haven't finished this one yet?' Nicole raised her eyebrows in Henry's direction. 'You got plans buster.'

'No plans, but I am sure the Prof has.'

Maggie felt herself blush and was relieved when Larry rescued the situation by telling everybody about the various tenants at the block of flats. He really got a kick out of the old biddy in the flat on the ground floor who took an interest in everybody's coming and goings. She had a strong English accent. It seemed the block had people there from all corners of the globe.

'My parents were both from Italy,' said Nicole, "and they weren't all that happy when I married an Irish bloke. At least he was a Catholic. We all come from somewhere, that's Australia for you. Not many of us can claim to have family been here for thousands of years."

'So how come you're not with your husband now?' asked Maggie. 'Was he a brute?'

'No.' Nicole teared up. 'He was a lovely guy; he died in an accident on a building site. Left me a widow with a three-year-old, well he's twelve now.'

'Oh dear. I am so sorry, that was a thoughtless question to ask,' said Maggie really embarrassed by her narrow view of marital life.

Much to her relief, the buzzing device Henry had brought to the table announced that their lunches were ready to be picked up at the bar. She and Larry went up to pick the plates up.

'Not quite what I imagined after seeing Jimmy's bedroom set up. She seems really nice,' Maggie whispered to Larry.

'Henry seems to think so too.' Larry chuckled. 'Still waters run deep my love.'

They carried the meals back to their table as Henry poured from the second bottle.

'That's it for me,' said Nicole as he went to top up her glass. 'My clapped-out car is already likely to draw the cops' attention; I can't afford to be caught driving over point- o- five.'

'You and me both, luv.' Henry looked suitably chastened. He had yet to tell Nicole of his past history of driving while intoxicated. 'Maggie can have some more and if there is any leftover, I reckon the bottle will fit in that big handbag of hers.'

Maggie did leave with the bottle in her bag thinking to herself that a bottle is a lot heavier than a few sausage rolls.

CHAPTER SIXTEEN

'Somewhere round here was where Bogle and Chandler were found,' Jess expounded as they raced down the hill towards Lane Cove National Park, in the northern suburbs of Sydney.

'Who the fuck's Bogle and Chandler?' replied Danny immediately regretting using the expletive in front of Jess. At times she made him feel dumb. She seemed too smart to be a copper and she certainly didn't fit the blond stereotype, that's for sure.

'It was a big mystery back in the early sixties. A couple having a bit of extramarital hanky-panky ended up dead on the riverbank down near Fullers Bridge. Nobody ever worked out how or why they died, although they appeared to be poisoned. I guess it was all considered scandalous back then.'

'Geez Jess. How do you know all this stuff?'

'It got mentioned in a lecture about the Coroners Court.'

'How's the study going?'

'Okay. I'm glad they put the lectures up on-line because it's so hard to attend regularly with the bloody shifts they put me on. You'd better slow down. The park entrance is coming up.'

Danny turned the patrol car into the park. The early morning walkers and joggers stared at the flashing lights as the car slowly made its way into the park. One poor bugger had come across a body in the water where the river formed a small lake. Some forward thinkers back in the past had built a weir to create a lake for the park.

It seemed pretty obvious that the lucky finder was the old guy waving frantically at them, down at the water's edge. He was getting a bit of extra exercise with his waving. They got out of the vehicle and walked over to the elderly gentleman. His track suit pants looked soaked and he was shivering.

'G'day. I'm glad you guys are here. I pulled him in before he went over or got caught in the weir,' he proudly explained.

'Thanks. You did the right thing. We'll get your details in a minute. If you could just wait over by the car while we check on the body,' said Jess pointing to the car with its red and blue lights still flashing. 'I'll get you an emergency blanket out of the boot in a sec or two.'

Danny was already squatting down by the corpse. 'Hey Jess, come and check this out and let me know what you think. Looks like this guy took a beating and I reckon it might be that prick we picked up three weeks ago for that road rage incident.'

'Bloody hell. You're right. I never forget a face, even if

it's been rearranged,' she said with a wry smile. 'I guess we'd better call homicide. This is beyond our pay grade.'

An hour later the peaceful atmosphere of the park had evaporated. The detectives and forensic crew had arrived and attempts had been made to close the park. Jess and Danny were asked to have a look around further upstream on this side of the river. Another couple of uniforms were sent around to the other side.

Danny had always found the Lane Cove National Park pretty amazing. It consisted of bushland either side of the Lane Cove River with plenty of tracks and picnic areas. Wildlife galore and it was so hard to believe it was only about ten kilometres from the centre of Sydney. At weekends it was packed with visitors, but early on a Tuesday morning there were only a few around.

They slowly drove up Riverside Drive checking in at each picnic area as they went. Three times they stopped joggers or walkers and asked for their contact details before asking them to leave the park. At a picnic ground called Carters Creek, Jess was quick to point out a Nissan Patrol in the parking area.

'Okay Danny, can you remember the rego of our friend,' her blue eyes challenging the besotted Senior Constable.

'Arhh. AJ 21 FB I think,' was the reply.

'Close. AJ 12 FB. No chocolates for you I'm afraid.'

'I think it's supposed to be no cigar.'

'Not these days. Smoking is bad for your health,' Jess kept up the banter.

Sure enough, as they got up close to the Nissan, Jess was right. That memory of hers was impressive. The plates matched those of Brian Bennington's vehicle. Danny parked about twenty metres away and they climbed out of the patrol car to investigate, pulling on latex gloves. The Nissan was unlocked and was not displaying any parking ticket on the dash. Minor panel damage appeared on the front of the driver's side.

'Boy, we're sure kicking some goals today. I'll tape the area off if you could call and let them know down at the lake what we've found,' Danny instructed as he retrieved the blue and white tape from the patrol car's boot.

Fifteen minutes later the detectives arrived and directed their uniformed colleagues back to their task of checking further upstream.

Danny was more than happy with having to spend the rest of the morning with Constable Jess MacDonald.

CHAPTER SEVENTEEN

'I reckon you really should divorce him Maggie,' suggested Nicole. 'You're struggling and he's back there in Sydney living in the house which is partly yours.'

'Nobody understands how violent he can be.' Maggie took a sip of her cappuccino. 'Honestly, I reckon he would kill me if he caught up with me.'

'You should at least get legal advice. It's just wrong.' Nicole wasn't going to drop the subject. 'There are free legal services.' She gave Maggie a smile. 'I know that I'm Italian but unfortunately I can't call on the Godfather to have him bumped off; I am afraid that's a myth.'

'I'll think about it,' said Maggie before she placed her hand before her mouth and giggled. 'I mean about the legal advice, not having him killed.'

A tram rumbling passed interrupted their conversation. They were having coffee at a street side table outside a coffee shop in Riversdale Road, not far from the Op shop that Maggie loved. Earlier they had browsed the wares offered by the shop, paying particular attention to the second-hand clothes with the fancy labels. There was no doubt the quality of people's donations reflected the wealthy neighbourhood. It was a week after they had met at lunch with the blokes. They had talked about the op shop and agreed to go there together.

'I might be poor as a church mouse, but for once I'm really happy. Larry really looks after me. I'm not interested in having anything to do with Brian.' Maggie shook her head. 'He can divorce me if he wants to, although he'll have a hard time finding me.'

'You're lucky then. Larry seems a nice guy. I miss my Patrick and if it hadn't been for the bit of superannuation he had, and life insurance attached to it, I would've really been in a pickle. I was able to pay off the home loan and my job keeps me and my boy Anthony in the essentials.' Nicole swirled the last of her long black before she drained her cup.

'What about Henry. He seems pretty keen?' enquired Maggie.

Nicole looked a little uncomfortable. She took the opportunity to wipe her lips with the paper napkin, folded it and placed it under her saucer.

'I will just take it slowly. I know my whole friendship with Jimmy must seem a bit sordid and I don't want him to get the wrong idea.' Nicole looked down and inspected her nails before she switched her gaze to something in the distance. 'With Jimmy it was just a complete escape from the real world for an afternoon. I'd often visit my mum in the nursing home on a Thursday morning, even though she no longer knows who I am. It's pretty depressing. An afternoon frolic was good medicine.'

'Jesus, none of us are in a position to judge, believe me.' Maggie couldn't help herself smile as she looked across at her new friend and recalled her own reaction on first seeing the bedroom in the flat with those satin sheets. It was hard to reconcile the two. 'Henry has been good to Larry and I have even learnt to accept that sleazy wink.'

Nicole broke into a laugh. 'As you say none of us is perfect. I think that dumb wink is just part of the big fella. You know he told me how he and Larry met in jail. It seems he has been able to get back to a normal life better than Larry.'

'Larry might have a better chance if he didn't have me to carry,' murmured Maggie. She spooned the last of the froth from her cup. The cappuccino had been a real treat.

'Well, you think about claiming what is rightfully yours. I'll come with you for support if you decide to get free legal advice,' said Nicole.

Maggie changed the subject back to their earlier Op shop bargains knowing Nicole was pleased with her purchases. Among them was a genuine Richmond Tigers football jumper she had bought for her football-crazy son, Anthony. The team's recent success had turned him into a fanatic according to his mother. Apparently, Jimmy had taken them both to a game in the MCG members' section. Maggie told Nicole how they could hear the roar of the crowd at the Grand Final at the flat in Hawthorn when Richmond thrashed Western Sydney, even though the MCG was probably five kilometres away. It had only been a couple of weeks ago and Anthony was still on a high according to Nicole.

As she walked back down Riversdale Road towards the flat Maggie thought over what Nicole had said. She and Brian had a home in Chatswood and like all of Sydney it was a valuable property. The title to the house was in Brian's name for business purposes. He used it as collateral for his property development projects. She knew Nicole was right and she should try divorcing him, but the thought terrified her. Wouldn't it be great if he just died? A heart attack, cancer or better still a car accident. Shame and disgust replaced these thoughts. It was truly troubling; how could she be so callous? She should be satisfied with the happiness she had found with Larry.

Her latest friend, Nicole had turned out to be a real surprise. Maggie had imagined that the women who had been the purpose of Jimmy's flat would have been glamourous party types. A sensitive, intelligent widow didn't fit the mould created in Maggie's mind. Her recent discovery of the joys of sex helped her understand why Nicole had been happy to relish those weekly sessions. For all those years Maggie had met her husband's demands with little pleasure. Still, it was not a time for regrets; she must live in the moment, after all she was as happy as she had ever been.

CHAPTER EIGHTEEN

Jess pulled on her tracksuit over her running gear. They had completed over ten kilometres according to the app on her phone and it would appear that Danny was feeling the effects more than she was.

Was this a date? She hadn't quite worked that out yet. When they had been searching through the park after finding Bennington's body they had been chatting about all sorts of things. On hearing Jess was a runner, Danny suggested they come back on a day off and run around the park. On the spur of the moment she agreed, assuming he was a serious runner.

A few days later, they met at the park and had set off from near the boatshed running up the riverside walking trail, then crossed De Burghs Bridge to return on the opposite side of the river. She chatted away at first, at the start of their run, but soon Danny was not able to keep up his side of the conversation. Aware that Danny might have overestimated his running ability, she slowed the pace a little. She even stopped to admire their audience of a half dozen rainbow lorikeets, while Danny sucked in the eucalyptus scented air. To his credit he made it the whole way without calling *uncle*.

Danny, having struggled into a windcheater, walked over to her tiny pink Fiat. He was carrying a near empty water bottle.

'Would you like to grab a cup of coffee at the Café? I'm afraid I'm not much of a conversationalist when I'm running.' He wiped the sweat from his forehead with his sleeve. 'I'm obviously not in your league.' He looked embarrassed. 'I mean about running.'

Jess giggled and punched him lightly on the arm. 'Sure. I've a bit of goss about that dead guy,' she replied as they walked towards the Café.

They bought their coffees and chose an outside table, making the most of the gentle breeze that helped them cool down from their exercise.

'I talked to that Colin guy in the homicide squad yesterday,' Jess divulged. 'It seems Bennington was out on bail. Somebody has given him a hiding and dumped him in the river. The post-mortem showed the cause of death was drowning.'

'Why were you speaking to that Colin guy?' quizzed Danny.

'None of your business,' she replied. *Was he jealous? Obviously, he didn't realise Colin was a balding fifty-year-old detective with a middle-aged gut.* 'If you really want to know; he just rang me because he thought I might be interested.

I guess he had my number from when I rang him about the Nissan we found the other day.'

'Oh yeah,' Danny sounded sceptical, 'anything else?'

'Yep. They are worried about his wife. The neighbours say they haven't seen her for years.'

'I think the backyard would be too rocky to bury her there from my memory of the house location,' he said.

'That's right, remember those bloody steps? Apparently, it's planned to put out an appeal on Crime Stoppers. The wife had an AVO out on him at one stage, so who knows what has happened. Someone's done her a favour if she's still in one piece.'

'Do they think the wife might have had him sorted?' asked Danny raising his eyebrows.

'More likely he has done something to her. She is a *person of interest* as they like to say for the media.'

'Well thanks for the update and the run; I've had a good time although I don't think my legs will agree about that tomorrow,' said Danny as they left the café.

'Likewise. We should do it again,' she said, although she thought perhaps a movie might be a better option.

CHAPTER NINETEEN

Gladys Gentry was at the venetian blinds as usual; just keeping an eye on what was happening in the block of flats. She was curious about the couple in the flat directly above theirs. She and Herb had been renting number eight for nearly ten years and this was the first time anybody had been living full time in number ten. Previously it seemed somebody was only there one or two days a week. That Mr O'Connor bloke and a few different women. Disgraceful goings on, for sure.

'Hey Glad, come away from the window. You're missing *The Bold and the Beautiful*. Brooke's up to her old tricks. She's gonna get married again.' Herb was tired of his wife's constant vigilance and obsession with the comings and goings outside.

'In a minute luv. Number ten is going somewhere. It's funny they don't have a car.' She replied. They appeared a happy couple. Could do with a decent feed. Much better having them living upstairs than having funny business going on.

'If you weren't my missus, 1 would call you a sticky beak. You know, it's probably a smart move not having a car. That bloody Camry costs us a packet just to have it sitting out the back. We only seem to use it for the weekly grocery run to Woolies' and your hair appointments.'

Larry and Maggie were no longer visible, so Gladys shuffled across to her recliner and joined Herb for the daily fix of their favourite soap.

'Stop your whinging, Herb; would you want me to look unkempt?' Gladys touched her coiffed hair which was holding up well, having been styled and set two days ago at Ricardo's Hair Salon. He was a magician as far as she was concerned, as somehow he enhanced what was once her crowning glory, with body and bounce, and an added shade of pale lavender.

Before the episode had reached its inevitable climax, Herb's eyes were shut as he dreamt of his younger more active days. It was Glady's squeal which brought him back to the present.

'It's her, I'm sure,' she shouted.

'What are you on about now?' Herb was less than impressed with the interruption to his slumbers.

'They just had one of those Crime Stopper things on the telly. They showed a photo of the woman in number ten. I'm sure it was her, although the photo must have been an old one as her hair was really red.'

'Oh yeah, sure, I suppose she's a bank robber,' cackled Herb.

'You don't believe me, do you?' Gladys was annoyed by his scepticism. 'Feel like making your own tea tonight?'

Silence settled over the living room except for the television shouting the benefits of stone-based cookware which came with a set of free knives.

In a matter of minutes Gladys could no longer keep what she had seen to herself.

'It didn't say she was dangerous, just that they were trying to trace her and were worried for her welfare. Seems her husband was killed.' She mused on this for a moment. 'I guess that means her little friend is not Mr Redhead, eh?'

'So, what you going to do, stick your beak in?' Herb was really leading with his chin.

'You're horrible sometimes! I'm going to do the right thing and ring the Crime Stopper number. So there!' Gladys poked her tongue out, something she hadn't done in years.

Herb had to laugh as she went into the hallway to the telephone. Never before had her continual surveillance of the neighbourhood amounted to anything other than a constant commentary.

The following day the venetians parted further than normal when the police car drove down to the back of the units. Gladys watched the two female police officers making their way to the doorway to her part of the building. She rushed to the front door and squinted through the security peep hole as she heard them climbing the stairs. They passed by on their way upstairs and she heard them ringing the doorbell of number ten. It was just so exciting and to think Herb was napping while this was happening. She hurried back to the living room to bring him up to date.

CHAPTER TWENTY

Larry opened his eyes and took a second or two to recall what he was doing high up in a truck cabin cruising along the Hume highway, winding through rolling hills. A sign indicated that the dog sitting on the tuckerbox was five kilometres ahead. He glanced across at Ryan, the young bloke driving; well, he was probably in his late thirties but to Larry everyone seemed young these days. He was smartly dressed in moleskins and a pale blue shirt with a company logo on its pocket.

'Hey there Larry, I see you're back with us mate. It's a pretty smooth ride, isn't it? All my passengers back there look pretty relaxed too, eh?' Ryan's eyes glanced up at the video screen which showed the horses riding in the purpose-built truck. 'Key part of this job is to maintain an even speed, avoid swapping lanes and no hitting the brakes, that way the horses can all keep their balance and relax.'

'Sorry about that, I guess I'm not used to an early start.

I can't remember much after Benalla; that's a serious nap,' replied Larry.

'Don't sweat it mate. I haven't needed your services. Do you really know your way round horses or was Henry bullshitting again?'

'He was a bit loose with the truth,' admitted Larry, 'but I'll give anything a crack if it gets me to Sydney.'

'Don't like flying, Larry?'

'Broke mate. It's a bit hard to get a job at my age plus there's a few issues.'

Larry was so glad Henry had managed to get him a lift with this bloke heading up to Randwick with three race-horses on board. They had left the stables at Cranbourne at five a.m. and had been on the road nearly seven hours.

'I'll be stopping up ahead at the famous dog on the tuck-erbox to check on my passengers and stretch our legs, eh?' said Ryan.

'That will be great, I could do with a leak,' replied Larry whose bladder was no longer as reliable as it once was.

So much had happened in the last few days. Two uniformed police officers turned up to inform Maggie about the death of her husband. It had been a huge shock. She hadn't done herself any favours by initially laughing hysterically as all those years of terror had come to an end. Larry tried to calm her down but was asked to go and make tea by the heavy-set chubby policewoman and he was followed into the kitchen by her younger female colleague. As the kettle boiled, she quizzed him as to who he was, his relationship with Maggie, how long they had lived at the flat and why his ID had a different address. The questions seemed to go on and on and all the time he could hear the senior officer trying to calm Maggie down and ask her questions. He made Maggie a sugary tea and asked the police if they would like a cuppa, which they declined.

Sergeant Chubby went into the hall and spent some time talking on her mobile phone. When she returned, she gave little information about the Brian bloke's demise, other than it appeared he was murdered. Maggie was *a person of interest* according to the New South Wales authorities. Larry had pleaded as to how ridiculous that was, as she had been nowhere near Sydney. His pleadings were ignored. They asked Maggie to pack a bag as more than likely she would be flown to Sydney. Sure enough, that is what had happened and had led to Larry hitching a ride with some fancy racehorses.

The truck started to slow ever so gently before turning into the famous rest stop. Larry was surprised when Ryan drove past the large complex consisting of a service station and fast foods. He gently cruised further down the road to where the historic bronze dog sat upon the tuckerbox.

'It's much quieter down here and we need to check on the horses,' said Ryan as he pulled to a stop. 'There's a loo over there behind the statue. You have a piss and then you can give me a hand.'

Larry being a man who could always follow instructions

returned to the truck after he had relieved his aging bladder. By this stage Ryan already had one of the compartments open and was topping up a feed bin for a beautiful looking horse. With a tilt of his head, he indicated a shovel attached to the side of the compartment. 'Grab that could you Larry and pop the poo in the bucket there.'

Larry chuckled to himself as now he literally had a shit job. He shovelled up the two dumplings and dropped them in the bucket. They repeated their respective tasks with the other two horses and Ryan locked up the truck.

'Okay, Larry, how about you stay here and keep an eye on things and I'll walk back to the Service Centre and get us a couple of burgers, my shout. I don't want to disturb the passengers and I need the exercise, eh. Another four hours and we will be in Sydney.'

'Sure. I can't argue with that. Thanks mate,' replied Larry. Ryan took off walking back up the hill to the massive modern Service Centre.

Larry studied the historical monument dating back to the nineteen thirties. It seemed such a remarkably small and simple thing compared with modern tourist attractions. It was nestled down in the valley five miles from Gundagai. Originally beside the highway it was now bypassed by a dual lane carriageway and most people who stopped probably didn't get past the flash service centre at the top of the hill. It was enough to make Larry feel his age, as if the world was changing too fast for him to keep up. He dreaded what could be waiting for him in Sydney and hoped that Maggie was okay. Just as they had become happy and settled, suddenly their world had gone tits up. He was so relieved when Maggie had left a text message on Jimmy's phone suggesting he get in touch with Henry. She had also left a Sydney phone number of someone called Amanda.

CHAPTER TWENTY-ONE

'It's Friday the sixth of December in the year twenty nineteen. Present are Margaret Bennington, Constable Jessica MacDonald and Senior Detective Colin Wilson. Mrs Bennington, you are the wife of Brian Bennington, is that correct?'

All the bluff and bullshitting had disappeared from Maggie. She was stunned by the last twenty-four hours. It was only yesterday the two cops had turned up at Hawthorn. Somehow, they had tracked her down to tell her about her husband Brian's death. She now wished she'd acted as the bereaved wife with tears and sadness. But how could she feel sad, instead she felt a huge relief that the cloud hanging over her life had blown away. Her relief manifested itself in hysterical laughter. Big mistake it would seem.

Here she was in a bare room, sitting at a crappy laminex table across from two cops. It was if she had suddenly been cast in a B grade movie or TV show,

'Yes, that's correct, but I escaped from him, to Melbourne, a couple of years ago, before he could kill me.'

'Mrs Bennington, did you have any contact with him in that time? Did you seek a divorce?'

'Please call me Maggie.' She didn't want to be known as Mrs. Bennington. 'I had no contact with him. I didn't want him to find me. He had promised to kill me. You should know that I had an intervention order out on him which he ignored. Fat lot of good that did!'

'We are aware of his violent tendency Maggie. But are you expecting us to believe that you made no attempt to collect some sort of financial support? You just left the house in Chatswood? Why didn't you attempt to get what you were legally entitled to?'

Suddenly the penny dropped. Maggie realised that in their eyes she had a financial motive to want Brian dead. Revenge for her previous abuse was possibly also considered a motive. Perhaps she had been a coward in not attempting to get a settled divorce, but all the money in the world is no good to you when you are a corpse.

'I have told you I was terrified of Brian.'

'Okay Maggie. Who is the bloke you are living with in Melbourne?'

'What's Larry got to do with this? Leave him out of it.' Her thoughts flashed to Larry who was in a bigger state of shock than she was when she was taken and put on a plane to Sydney. She had avoided arrest by cooperating in coming to Sydney.

'Is his name Larry Jenkins?' asked the detective.

'Yes, it is, but we've been in Melbourne the whole time, so this has nothing to do with us.'

'Do you realise that your mate Larry has a criminal record?'

'Sure, he told me he got into strive by doing some dodgy bookwork at a place he was working at. He's learnt his lesson, done his time. Give the man a break.'

'How do you know he hasn't got some mates up here in Sydney that would do the pair of you a favour?'

Maggie looked at Constable MacDonald who rolled her eyes when she caught Maggie's glance. Jess had picked her up at Mascot airport, waiting at the gate. When Maggie had expressed her horror at walking through the terminal with a police officer, Jess had told her to smile and pretend she had a daughter who was a cop. So, Maggie proceeded to loudly tell her about an imaginary Uncle Bob. Jess had laughed and seemed to enjoy the game. She had even helped Maggie contact her old friend Amanda. Constable Jess MacDonald was a good stick as far as Maggie was concerned.

The portly, balding detective was a different matter. He seemed to have made his mind up that Maggie was somehow involved in Brian's death. How the hell that had happened she had no idea.

'Have you ever had any contact with the Black Rebels bikie gang?'

Maggie stifled a laugh. 'I am in my very late fifties for God's sake. Do I look like a bikie's moll?'

'I asked if you ever had contact. I wasn't suggesting you were a bikie?'

'No, I have never had contact with bikies.'

'What about Larry Jenkins? He ever mentioned anything about bikie mates?'

'No, he hasn't. Why this obsession with bikies, if I might ask a question?'

Wilson considered this for a moment before he replied. 'We believe that Brian Bennington, your husband, was murdered. Bashed and drowned, possibly by a bikie gang. They have been known to kill for money. Did you authorise a hit on your husband?'

It sounded ludicrous to Maggie and when she looked across at her pretend daughter, she too was trying to keep a straight face. 'That's ridiculous. I don't have any money and I wouldn't have a clue how to organise such a thing.'

'Your friend Larry might have organised it.'

'Believe me Larry's not the organising type. Leave him out of this. Just find who killed my husband.' Maggie paused and looked directly at the detective. 'It's true that I'm not greatly upset that he's dead, but for God's sake, I had nothing to do with his death.'

Detective Wilson looked down at his notepad and, rubbed his hand across his bald head as if he was smoothing down a full head of hair. He then looked up and stared at

Maggie before taking on a new line of questioning. 'Tell me about your husband's business dealings.'

'Gee, I can't help you much there. I've been in Melbourne for the last two years. He considered himself a property developer for the last ten or so years. Only small stuff really. Buy some house on a decent size block he could knock down, then manage the building of some town houses.' Maggie paused while Wilson scratched something on his notepad. 'I haven't a clue about the last year or so.'

'Did he ever have trouble with the building unions?' asked Wilson.

'Not that I know of. Look he didn't share much with me. I was just supposed to sit at home and be a housewife. Make sure his dinner was on the table, his shirts ironed, keep everything clean. He'd give me a thump or two if things weren't right. I hated it when his development was out west because the traffic would get him in a right state.'

Jess could no longer keep quiet. 'Gosh, Colin, he sounds like a pretty unstable man. I witnessed his anger firsthand when Danny Lee and I arrested him over that road rage incident. He could've got on the wrong side of anyone.'

'Thanks for your insight, Constable MacDonald,' Wilson said sarcastically without even looking at her. 'Interview suspended at 6.05 pm. Would you see to Mrs Bennington please Constable.'

With that the Detective picked up his notepad and left.

Jess smiled at Maggie and said, 'Don't worry too much.

It's just his manner. You said you were going to stay with a friend. If you don't mind going in a divvy van, I can give you a lift if it's in your old neighbourhood. You will have to stay around while the investigation is going on.'

'That would be very kind. She doesn't live far away. You won't get into trouble, will you?'

'No. it's all good. I have to get your address and contact details in any case. Come on, grab your bag.'

CHAPTER
TWENTY-TWO

This definitely felt like a date. Danny had asked her what she was doing on her night off and suggested they go out for dinner as he was not on a late shift. He had suggested an Italian Pizzeria in the centre of Chatswood and Jess was quite happy to indulge herself with some pasta. She had even slipped on a dress rather than wearing her favourite jeans. The suggestion of Italian cuisine had surprised her at first as she half expected that they would be going to a Chinese restaurant, but then she was shocked at herself for her racial stereotyping of her colleague. Was Danny's heritage subconsciously an issue for her? It was something she may have to ponder in the future.

Danny took one look at her as they met up outside the restaurant and blurted out, 'Jess, you look too classy for this joint. We should have gone to somewhere really upmarket.'

'Next time,' she replied with a grin, 'It's a bit different from the uniform, I know.'

They were shown to their table and after a quick study of the menu ordered their meals and a bottle of a Hunter Valley Shiraz.

It didn't take long, after a little small talk, the conversation drifted back to the job.

'See that detective, Colin, has roped you in with that murder investigation with the missing wife?' Danny said in between mouthfuls of his ravioli.

'He has given me some of the hack work. When he found out about my studies, I think he has cast himself in a mentor role. I had to pick up the poor woman from the airport and drive her back for an interview at the station. He had me sit in on the interview.'

'What's he like?' Danny was suspicious of this bloke taking an interest in Jess. He leaned forward with a frown rarely seen on his face.

'I don't think he's the sharpest knife in the drawer. Seriously, he was banging on as if this poor woman had ordered a hit on her prick of a husband. Since when is a hit carried out with a bashing and drowning? Heat of the moment thing if you ask me. But what do I know?'

'Well, I reckon you're pretty smart. Why does he think it was a hit?" queried Danny.

'Well apparently the damage on his vehicle had traces of paint matched to a Harley Davidson model. Colin straight away decided bikies. The poor woman who has been hiding in Melbourne was sharing with an ex-con. Join the dots.'

'Sounds like a stretch to me,' said Danny returning to his ravioli.

'More likely another road rage incident in my opinion. Honestly the woman said she only had a little money, couldn't even afford a mobile phone; she had to use a payphone at the airport to contact an old friend for a place to stay. I don't know why she agreed to fly up here to Sydney; they must have put the pressure on her in Melbourne.' Jess paused to take a sip of her wine. 'Colin did think that her poverty was motive enough to want him murdered. Presumably if she is still married, she would have a pretty good chance of getting the house and any money the bastard had.'

'This Colin sounds a bit old school to me. Happy to mentor a young looker but not much sympathy for an older woman who been bashed by her husband. I thought the force had moved on a bit from that type.'

'Oh, I'm a looker am I? You know it may not be my looks that got me involved. Colin knows I'm studying Criminology.' Jess was pleased with the compliment on one hand but not pleased by his overlooking her ambition and intellect.

'Yeah sure. I know his type. Just watch yourself.'

'You're not jealous, are you? Getting kind of protective,' teased Jess before she realised it suggested a step further in their relationship.

'Do you think you'll be kept in the loop? Will the

powers-that-be let this Colin bloke second you at will?

'I hope so. I think ultimately that I'd like to get out of uniform and become a detective. What about you Danny?

'I'm not sure. I've been thinking of trying my luck in the country somewhere. Get out of Sydney and be the local cop somewhere.'

Jess was speechless for a moment. It did seem that they had quite different aspirations. Still, that's the future; she could add that to the list of things she needed to think about.

CHAPTER TWENTY-THREE

Amanda was almost in tears as she welcomed Maggie into her home. 'Oh Maggie, why didn't you let us know where you were and that you were okay? I've been so worried about you.' She threw her arms around Maggie's scrawny body and drew her into a hug against the extra kilos she carried on her short frame. 'I don't know what to say about Brian's murder. I can't imagine what trouble he had got himself into. Did you know he was due in court over a road rage incident? That bloody temper of his.'

'I'm so sorry if I caused you worry but I was terrified he would find me. I kept my whereabouts secret from everyone. It's been difficult, but luckily, I've been looked after by a nice bloke who I met.' Maggie paused for a moment and shrugged her shoulders 'Well, I suppose we really looked after each other.'

Amanda twiddled with her bright red, dangling earrings.

'Where is this bloke? What's his name? He's not here looking after you now, is he? I'm happy for him to stay here too if he's a friend of yours.'

Maggie blushed. 'Larry's his name. He's a bit more than a friend if you know what I mean. He's trying to get up here somehow. It's a bit tricky because we are short of money most of the time. I gave him your number.'

'Don't you have a mobile phone? What do you mean you are short of money? Brian seemed to have been doing okay. This is crazy; we'll have to get you sorted.' Amanda hated injustice and loved to take on a cause. She may be seventy years old but that was not going to stop her going into battle.

'No more questions please Amanda. I've spent the whole afternoon answering questions. I think they are suggesting I had Brian bumped off. I'm sorry for disappearing and I swear I had nothing to do with Brian's murder.'

'Sometimes I think Cops watch too much TV,' said Amanda shaking her head, rattling those pendulous earrings. 'Blind Freddie could see you're not a killer! You really need legal representation by the sound of things.' Amanda's face broke into a smile as the solution was obvious. 'Janet's daughter might help. You remember Janet from book club? Heavy eyebrows, thick glasses, hardly said boo, tendency to hum to herself.'

'Whoa! I can't afford to pay a solicitor.'

'Let me worry about that. I'm sure Brian will have some money that you can gain access to, not to mention the house.'

Amanda was in her organising mode and things were going to happen. She marched Maggie off to the spare room and ran the bath in the guest's bathroom. Maggie was exhausted and happy to follow instructions.

As Maggie soaked in the bath relishing in the luxury of the scented bath salts, she reflected on how so much had taken place in such a short space of time. She had been so happy in Hawthorn, happier than she had been in years. It had been a Spartan existence, but she had been content. Now with Brian's death everything had been turned on its head. Or had it? Nicole had encouraged her to seek what she was rightfully entitled to, but nobody could have ever anticipated these circumstances. She felt guilty regarding her feelings. She was so glad that her husband was dead. What was wrong with her? She should make an effort to hide her feelings. Perhaps take on the role of the upset, grief-stricken widow, after all she was a master of bullshit.

She dried herself off with the large fluffy bath sheet before dressing in her pyjamas and a large, well-worn towelling bath robe Amanda had supplied. Amanda had ordered in some Thai food delivered by a guy on a motor scooter. Maggie had not realised how hungry she was after her ordeal and she ate heartily ignoring the coriander dominating the food, a herb she normally disliked. Together as they ate, they filled each other in on what their lives had involved in the years Maggie had spent in hiding, before Maggie called it a night.

The guest bed was comfortable enough, but Maggie could not get to sleep. How she missed Larry spooning her. Would he come to Sydney as he had promised? Would things still be the same between them? Could she really inherit the house? What was the state of Brian's finances? Was there any money? Eventually, with the doubts and questions still unanswered Maggie fell into a restless sleep.

CHAPTER TWENTY-FOUR

'Maggie? Are you awake? Your Larry's on the landline. Apparently, he's made it up to Sydney. You better get up girl and talk to the poor man. He's lucky I answered as we only seem to get tele-marketing calls and scammers on the landline.'

'Oh, he's a darling, I wonder how he got here,' said Maggie as she slid out of bed. She wrapped herself in Amanda's bath-robe and followed her into the hall.

'Hello, Larry?'

'Maggie, I've made it up to Sydney and I'm currently in Randwick. I hitched a ride with some horses. Where are you? I'll work out how to get there.'

'What do you mean you rode on a horse? Have you been drinking already?'

'No, the horses were in a truck, real flash truck. Henry organised it. I stayed over at the stables last night. I helped with a few jobs after we arrived. Are you okay? The cops didn't lock you up?'

'The detective is a dickhead. I don't see how I could've been responsible for Brian's death, being in Melbourne,' she replied.

'Am I able to stay with you?' asked Larry.

'Amanda said you could stay here.'

'Where's here? You'd better give me the address and I'll find my way there.'

'Oh, I am so glad you got here Larry. I've been really stressed by everything; I'll tell you all about it when you get here. Hang on and I'll get Amanda to give you directions,' said Maggie before she went to find her host.

Amanda didn't hesitate to go to the phone. She reassured Larry he was welcome and gave him directions. It was pretty obvious that this couple definitely needed a mobile phone and she decided to add that to her to do list. Maggie was really in need of a bit of sound judgement and protection from the circumstances that had surrounded her. Amanda was about to take her under her wing.

'Maggie, help yourself to tea and toast in the kitchen. I'm going to ring Janet and get her daughter's number; I'm sure she will help you.'

In no time Amanda had the wheels in motion, Maggie was going to get access to what was rightfully hers.

Larry had advice from the stable hands who had provided him with an Opal card with a little credit left on it. This was courtesy of some inebriated race goer. Apparently, it was not unusual for the punters to lose all sorts of valuables by the end of a race meeting. One young stable hand had consulted his smart phone. He explained to Larry, *the old bloke from Melbourne*, that he was to catch a bus to Central Station where he could get a train to Chatswood. They wished him luck as he headed to the bus stop with his sports bag of clothes.

When Maggie heard the front gate's hinges squeal announcing Larry's arrival, she rushed to the front door and flung it open.

'I guess I've found the right joint then,' said Larry with a broad smile. He looked bedraggled and had a smell about him of straw and manure. Despite this Maggie threw her arms around him and burst into tears. 'Hey! I know I might be a sight for sore eyes, but it can't hurt them that much. Dry those pretty blue eyes,' Larry said gently.

Amanda appeared at the doorway. 'Come in Larry and I'll get you settled in. Maggie's been having a rough time and she's obviously pleased to see you.'

By this time, Maggie took a deep breath and wiped her tears away with the back of her hand. She led Larry to the bathroom and presenting him with a towel said, 'Okay Stinky. You jump in the shower, clean yourself and we can exchange stories when you're presentable. I'll stick your clothes in the washer.'

Twenty minutes later, a spick and span Larry was formally introduced to Amanda and over a cup of tea he related his saga; the travelling to Sydney with the thoroughbred horses and bunking down in the stables overnight. Maggie told her story of the flight to Sydney and the harrowing interview. It was only then that Amanda announced that Janet's daughter Stephanie had agreed to represent Maggie without charge at this stage, but that might change if Maggie's circumstances recover.

'She obviously thinks your financial position will improve,' chuckled Amanda. 'She's going to pop around and meet you after work if you're happy with that' The two women exchanged looks and nodded in agreement. Larry could only shrug and smile, this really was not his decision to make.

'How could I not be. Do you think I will be able to gain access to the house?' asked Maggie.

'Time will tell, my dear,' replied Amanda, 'I'll let her know that you're in agreement with the arrangements. When I'm all done, we'll go up to the Telstra shop and organise a mobile phone for the pair of you.'

In no time she had her visitors out the door and into her five-year-old Volvo and her mission had commenced.

CHAPTER TWENTY-FIVE

At a little after five o'clock the doorbell rang and Amanda answered it. There was no mistaking Janet's daughter. Sure, she was obviously younger, but her face was almost identical, and she too wore thick glasses, albeit a stylish pair with thick blue frames. It was there the similarities ended for whereas Janet rarely said a word her daughter Stephanie was confident and articulate.

'You must be Maggie,' she said firmly shaking Maggie's hand. 'I am sorry about your husband's death although I understand you had your differences.'

'I've spent the last two years hiding in Melbourne. He had become a violent man and had threatened to kill me, and he meant it! It was much more than differences. But I promise you I had nothing to do with his death. The police have this crazy idea that I had something to do with it. Like, I ordered a hit on him!' Maggie paused for a minute before she grabbed

Larry's hand. 'This is Larry. We have been living together in Melbourne. What better alibi could I have?'

'Who knows how they think? I guess they think you have a motive. It's hard to imagine you would wait two years and as you say, you hardly had an opportunity to do anything living in Melbourne.' Stephanie pushed her glasses back up her nose and looked at Maggie directly. 'From now on I want you to act as a bereaved widow. You remember those good times you had?' Understand what I mean?' She smiled at Maggie and continued. 'I will approach the police and make sure that you can gain access to the marital home, and demand that any of your husband's personal items are handed over. The car will probably be kept as evidence for a while. What about his body? You will most likely be expected to make arrangements with funeral directors.'

'Brian's funeral? Shit. You've got to be kidding.' Maggies blue eyes were blazing.

'Bereaved widow remember; it will make things easier,' counselled Stephanie.

'Well, you can bet I'll have the bastard cremated that's for sure,' said Maggie, 'Give him a taste of hell.'

Stephanie then proceeded to ask whether he had a will. Whose name was the house in? Bank accounts? Did Maggie know who his solicitor was?

Stephanie kept the questions coming recording their conversation on her smart phone. It seems the days of the pen and notebook had passed.

Maggie answered as best she could and felt sure her answers could be confirmed if they were able to get into the house and go through Brian's office. Stephanie would see what she could do about the house, but as tomorrow was Saturday, she wasn't making any promises. They gave her the number of their new mobile phone and she reassured them not to worry. And with that she left.

'My God, can you believe that about the body?' Maggie was shaking. 'How am expected to pay for that.'

Amanda placed a hand on her shoulder. 'Don't worry about that. He'll pay for his own funeral; it will come out of his estate. Let's all have a drink before we have dinner.'

In no time at all Amanda had a bottle of white wine out of the refrigerator and was filling up three glasses. Larry took his glass but said nothing as he tried to take in all that had been happening. He felt sure someone would tell him eventually what was expected of him.

CHAPTER TWENTY-SIX

Larry rolled over out of bed and headed for the bathroom. Birds outside were excitedly discussing the day in front of them as the early morning sunlight forced its way through the trees. He must have slept well as this was his first bathroom visit for the night. Maggie was still snoring gently when he slid back under the doona. His mind went back over all that had happened. Certainly, he wanted to keep his distance from the cops but wanted to help Maggie as much as he could. If she was to play the role of the grieving widow, perhaps it would be the best if he slunk back to Melbourne.

It was hard to imagine what had happened to her jerk of a husband. Somebody had killed him. It was obvious he had shown he was violent and perhaps he just came off second best in a blue. He was glad he hadn't agreed to anything when Henry had suggested he knew people in Sydney who could sort the bludger out. He was sure Henry was bullshitting.

These thoughts danced through his mind as he drifted back off to sleep.

There was a knock on the door. 'Are you two ready for a cuppa and some toast? I have some news.'

Larry looked at his watch stunned that it was already after nine o'clock. He made his way to the bathroom once again and when he returned to the bedroom, he found Maggie was awake and dressing.

'How's my stable hand this morning?' she said giving him a peck on the cheek.

'Ready to put my head in the feedbag,' he replied as he attempted to take her in his arms.

'No time for kisses now. Get dressed and I will see you in the kitchen,' she said as she gently pushed him aside and left the room.

Larry naturally did as he was told and pulled on a clean pair of jeans and a flannelette shirt. Perhaps a bit down market for the northern suburbs of Sydney but his choices were limited. He headed to the kitchen.

Amanda poured him a cup of tea and announced, 'Stephanie rang me earlier. She said she had tried your number without success. It seems she made contact with the police and they have no objection with you having access to the house as they have already searched it for evidence. They have keys which were found in Brian's car. They can be picked up on Monday. So, I guess you will just have to be patient.'

Maggie passed the old fashion toast rack to Larry. He took a piece of toast wondering what they could do during the weekend. He was down to his last thirty dollars. His wondering soon finished when Maggie said, 'I bet the spare key is still hidden by step eighty-two. I think we should take a look.' She paused and took in Larry's puzzled expression. 'You'll understand when you see the house. There are one hundred and three steps to the front door. Lots of rocks to hide keys under.'

'I'll give you a lift around there when we have finished our breakfast 'said Amanda struggling to lift herself from the kitchen chair, before she took her dishes to the sink.

Fifteen minutes later they were in the Volvo and in another ten pulled into the carport at the bottom of Maggie's former home. The hundred and three steps were waiting.

'I don't think I'll climb the steps with you,' said Amanda. 'You ring me on your phone and let me know if you have found the key and got in.'

Larry followed Maggie up the steps and he could feel his heart rate increasing. It wasn't just from the physical effort but also from anxiety as to where their life was heading. Close to the house Maggie reached beside the stone steps and overturned a rock and gleefully held up a key ring. She took off up the remaining steps. Larry looked up at the house that appeared to be perched above them; a timber construction clad in weathered western red cedar, with large picture windows. The blue and white police tape draped across the front porch was easily ripped aside by Maggie, the key inserted and the front door opened.

'I'll let Amanda know,' said Larry as he pulled out their new smart phone. Maggie had already entered her old home. Would she want to stay here in Sydney? Larry put his concerns aside and let Amanda know of their success.

CHAPTER TWENTY-SEVEN

Maggie pushed open the door of what had been her home for twenty odd years. It seemed different than she remembered; it didn't smell the same and it was dirty and untidy. Obviously, her housewife skills had been missed. The view out of the large living room windows was the only thing that seemed to stir something within her. She picked up an empty pizza box and headed to the kitchen.

'Amanda said to ring when we want to be picked up. Jesus, can I help you with this mess luv?' Larry appeared at the door behind her as she surveyed the disaster.

'Let's leave it for a bit and have a look at the rest of the house,' she replied. 'Come on, upstairs. This way. There is really only the living room and kitchen on this level and a toilet, sorry powder room, and the laundry.'

'More bloody steps,' grumbled Larry. 'No wonder you are in such good health for a mature woman.'

"Watch it sunshine. Enough of the mature woman.'

Three bedrooms and a full bathroom occupied this upper level of the split-level home. One of the bedrooms was set up as Brian's office. They looked in and were surprised by how tidy and ordered it was compared with downstairs.

"Later, you should see what you can find out about his financial affairs on his computer.' said Maggie as she poked her head into the guest bedroom. She thought back as to how few times somebody had stayed over, a waste of space really. She had used the built-in wardrobe to store some of her clothes. She had a quick look and was surprised they were still there, albeit a bit on the musty side.

"I guess he thought I might come back,' she muttered.

The master bedroom was a different kettle of fish. A pile of dirty clothes graced the carpet at the foot of the unmade bed. Drawers were open and the built-in robe was open and in disarray. But still her clothes were there, pushed to one end.

'Okay Larry, I'm going to start cleaning up downstairs. Why don't you test your detective skills in Brian's office? See if you can find out if he is broke or worth a fortune. He seemed to always be on the computer,' she said, giving Larry a peck on the cheek as she pushed him towards the office.

Downstairs she threw herself into her old role as a domestic goddess. In the living room she picked up all the rubbish scattered around, straightened the furniture dusted every surface before she fetched the vacuum cleaner from the laundry cupboard.

Larry shouted from upstairs, 'The computer is password protected. Any clues? What was his birthday? What's his middle name? That sort of stuff.'

Maggie climbed the stairs trying to remember what he used as a password.

'His birthday was on February thirteen and he was born in 1959,' she recalled. Larry's fingers danced across the keyboard. before he shook his head.

"We were married on April second, 1980. Try that,' Maggie suggested.

Once again Larry tried different combinations. 'Bingo,' he shouted gleefully, 'I'll let you know what I've found out later. You can go back to work Sadie.'

Maggie giggled and gave him a playful punch. 'I hope the noise of the Dyson doesn't distract you from your work Prof, 'she said before she descended the stairs and fired up the vacuum cleaner. Despite doing what she had always done, this did not feel like home, in fact, she decided she would never want to live here again. The horror of her marriage haunted this house.

Two hours later when she had both the living room and the kitchen in reasonable order, she made tea and summoned Larry.

'Here's a cuppa love. What did you find out Sherlock?' she said as they settled on a sofa.

Larry had been occupied finding his way through Brian's computer records. His desktop computer was all well organised with records of correspondence, spreadsheets for various projects and a fairly simple accounting package. Larry was not familiar with this software but soon figured how it operated.

As he moved his mouse around Brian's home screen he had clicked on an icon on the favourite's taskbar he didn't recognise. It led to a website that appeared to offer a selection of pornographic video clips. His curiosity got the better of him and he clicked on *Plumber to the Rescue*. In no time at all, the plumber had the innocent looking housewife writhing naked on the floor while his apprentice tended to the leaking sink. When her ecstatic screams filled the room Larry quickly closed the link glad that the vacuum cleaner downstairs had covered up his digressions from the task at hand. No wonder Brian didn't trust Maggie near tradesmen if he watched this rubbish. He decided he would keep Brian's secret for the moment, Maggie had enough to worry about.

'Come on, spill the beans,' said Maggie.

'Well,' said Larry. 'It seems Bennington Developments has two projects on the go at the moment; a couple of town-houses at someplace called Greenacre which must be nearly finished and a vacant site at Merrylands that is waiting on council approval of some kind. It seems that this house carries a nine hundred thousand mortgage, so I guess it's worth more than that.'

He paused to sip his tea. 'I looked through the correspondence in the filing cabinet and have noted down the name of the solicitor he used. The solicitor might know if there is a will. The other thing you might not know is that you are a director of Bennington Developments.'

'Bloody hell, what do I know about the business? He used to sometimes make me sign stuff for tax purposes.' Maggie looked as if she was about to have another panic attack.

'Don't worry about it. We'll get Stephanie to sort it out. She seems to really know her stuff,' said Larry in his attempt to sooth Maggie's rising stress levels. He couldn't make a cup of tea this time as they were already drinking one. 'I can't be sure about the financial aspects, but it looks as if the company is solvent. The other thing is he has a self- managed superannuation fund; but that's a bit beyond my expertise.'

Maggie started to relax a little. 'Thanks Larry. I don't know what I would do without you.'

'I thought you might want to pick up on your old life. You'll have your house back and some money. I didn't know whether I should piss off back to Melbourne once things here are all organised,' said Larry studying the tea leaves in the bottom of his cup.

'Is that what you want? I love you, you dill. If you go back to Melbourne, I'm coming with you.' said Maggie with tears welling up.

'I just thought, you know, that things had changed. Of course, I love you Maggie Claymore, but I feel like I don't belong here,' said Larry trying not to put his foot in his mouth.

'I don't belong here anymore either, so just stop talking nonsense,' was her reply, sliding over the sofa and embracing Larry.

They stared out the picture windows at the view, neither sure of where their lives were heading but knowing that they were both heading there together.

CHAPTER
TWENTY-EIGHT

By the time Monday morning arrived the house had been cleaned completely. Larry had learnt as much as he could about Bennington Developments and a thorough search of the office had not found a will. Maggie had rediscovered many of her clothes and had even found her jewellery box untouched. Brian had always liked showering her with bling, often as an apology for a beating. She decided she would see if she could sell some of the pieces at *Cash Convertors*. They could do with extra cash, despite the fact that she had found about fifteen hundred dollars in a Tupperware container in the freezer.

They were still staying at Amanda's and Stephanie called soon after breakfast and suggested they meet at a nearby coffee shop prior to going to visit the police.

'Thanks for taking me on, Stephanie,' said Maggie. They had chosen a table in a quiet corner of the café. 'We were able to get into my old home over the weekend and Larry found out a bit about Brian's business. He's good with computers you know. I'll let him tell you what he found out.' Larry was up at the counter ordering the coffees.

'While we wait, I'll fill you in on what I found out from that detective Wilson. He was almost apologetic about how they had treated you when I got stuck into him. We can pick up some keys and personal effects that were found on your late husband's body. He thinks his remains will be available for the funeral directors by Wednesday.' Stephanie adjusted her thick blue framed spectacles before she continued. 'As the widow it is assumed you will be making the arrangements.'

Maggie was speechless for a moment; she was truly out of her depth.

'Don't worry, nobody knows what to do. Once you contact funeral directors, they guide you through the entire process. The other thing we need to find out is whether your late husband had a will,' said Stephanie.

At this stage Larry returned with two cappuccinos and a long black for Stephanie.

"Thanks Larry. We are talking about a possible will.' Stephanie tentatively sipped at her hot coffee before she continued. 'If he died intestate there are steps we will have to through, but at least then the money will come your way, under New South Wales law, unless there are children you don't know about.'

Larry realised it was time for him to divulge what he had discovered.

'I searched his file cabinet and couldn't find a will, but I do have the contact details of the solicitor he used for his business. In fact, they must have been mates because he even has a small share in the business.' Larry was enjoying sharing his findings. 'It seems our Maggie here is now the sole director of Bennington Developments, given that Mr Bennington is dead. She appears to be only a minor shareholder. She knew nothing of any of this.'

Larry continued explaining to Stephanie all he had discovered about the projects, the mortgage on the Chatswood home and the various bank accounts. All this time the stress was getting to Maggie and she looked as if she was about to cry. She really did look like a grieving widow.

There was no way Larry was going anywhere near the police, so he climbed those one hundred and three stairs and continued his research on what appeared to be the company that was now in Maggie's control. Stephanie had accompanied the grieving widow to see the boys in blue and they returned about two hours later. Maggie was dropped off at the house and by the time she reached the top of the steps she looked flushed and somewhat bedraggled.

'I haven't lost it,' she boasted. 'I really got into my role. I shed a tear and demanded that they find out who killed

Brian. The detective who was so mean to me before was dumbfounded. He handed me Brian's personal possessions. A drowned wallet which had his licence, a credit card and thirty-five dollars and his keys. The SUV is still held as evidence and to top it all off I am expected to arrange the funeral.'

'That won't be a problem,' said Larry, remembering Stephanie's advice. 'We will just contact some funeral directors and they will organise it. I reckon we should contact the *White Ladies*; you know those all-female funeral directors. A touch of irony. Eh?'

That was enough to get a giggle out of Maggie. 'I like that idea. By the way, Stephanie has been in contact with Brian's solicitor, a Shane Peterson. She wants us to go and meet him tomorrow. We will see what we can do to wind up the company. Will you come along?'

'Of course, Madam Director.' Larry desperately tried to lighten the mood. He couldn't imagine where the next few weeks would lead them.

CHAPTER TWENTY-NINE

'Come in, take a seat.' Shane Peterson ushered the three of them into what appeared to be an attempt at a conference room. A large antique dining table surrounded by six uphol-stered chairs was in the centre of the room. Stephanie sat between Larry and Maggie and Shane took up a chair oppo-site them and he placed a manila file on the table. He was a man in his late forties who had lost control of his waistline. Thick blond hair adorned his head; hair which would make any surfer proud.

'Maggie, I feel as if I know a bit about you. Brian had you down as a director of his company and of course also as a shareholder. He has been searching the country for you much of the last two years. He had me hire two private detectives. I've known Brian a long time and am aware of his temper, so I'm not about to judge.'

'If I could speak for Maggie, please', said Stephanie. 'We

need to know whether her late husband had a will and the state of his affairs.' She looked across at Maggie who looked as if she was about to cry. Was it an act? Stephanie wasn't sure.

'Absolutely. On the subject of the will, the answer is no. He was a stubborn bastard.' Shane looked directly at Maggie's tear-filled blue eyes. 'Sorry Maggie, but it's true. I advised him many times that he needed a will. With regard to the business, to the best of my knowledge it's solvent. Shitload of debt, but a couple of great assets.'

'So, what do you think is Maggie's best course of action? From what I understand she is now the sole director of Bennington Developments and only a minor shareholder, ten percent I believe?' queried Stephanie.

'I should disclose that I am also a minor shareholder.' stated Shane running his hand through his blond mane. Maggie and Larry faked surprised looks on their faces despite Larry's forensic efforts having already discovered this. 'He gave me a share as payment when the company was set up, but he has never paid out a dividend. I guess he screwed me on that deal.' Shane opened his folder and continued. 'It should not be difficult to sell the block which is cleared ready for development in Merrylands and the townhouses in Greenacre are at the final painting and land-scaping. Just weeks away from completion as long as you can pay the subcontractors. I am sure we can work together to wind up the company.' Shane pulled another sheet of paper out of the manila file. 'Look I've done a back of the envelope calculation earlier. Strikes me that by the time we sell the Merrylands block, complete and sell the units in Greenacre and clear the debt, the company should have about nine hundred thousand. My ten percent and maggies ten would leave over seven hundred going into the estate.'

Maggie looked towards Larry. 'What do you reckon my friend?'

'All sounds about right from what I could work out from the records. Seven hundred and ninety grand would pay off the mortgage on the house, if you decided to keep it.' Larry was a bit shocked to be consulted in front of the solicitor. 'The decision's all yours Maggie.'

'Are you happy with Shane and myself organising this Maggie,' enquired Stephanie. 'Ultimately the money in the estate will flow back to you if he died intestate.'

'Unless there are children we don't know about,' interrupted Shane, once again running his hand over his blond hair.

Maggie smiled for the first time. 'That's highly unlikely; we tried for years and I was checked out. Wasn't my problem.'

'Well, there are legal steps that must be gone through when a deceased dies intestate, so it will take some time.' Shane stuffed his papers back into the folder. 'You will let me know about the funeral, won't you?'

The meeting concluded and it was agreed that Shane would get the ball rolling with regard to disposing of the company's assets.

CHAPTER THIRTY

Larry stood towards the back of the room away from the table where they caterers had spread out the food. Another funeral where he didn't know the deceased. Just like old times. Maggie was holding up well. She did seem genuinely upset or was she just stressed by the whole pretence of being the widow. Amanda and Stephanie were close buy. Only about twenty other people turned up and seemed to be mainly blokes with the exception of Janet and a couple of Maggie's other book club friends. Larry presumed the rest were probably tradies or sub-contractors who the dearly departed had dealt with, a couple of neighbours perhaps. Apparently, he had no family except a few cousins in Western Australia.

The funeral directors, lovely ladies, had organised a celebrant who gave the briefest of eulogies. What a laugh, she was a woman too. Pretty funny given he was a wife beater. Maggie had given her a few details about Brian but left that bit out. She insisted that he had wanted a simple funeral, no fuss. His body was already on its way to the crematorium; it had been carted out once the short ceremony was over.

A man, dressed in more black than Johnny Cash, with a tattoo around his neck, moved next to Larry. He was armed with a stubby of Four X in one hand and a paper plate of food in the other. The stubby was placed at his feet and he took a bite out of a sausage roll. 'Pretty good spread, yeah? Love a good sausage roll,' he said with crumbs of pastry joining the stubby at his feet. 'How'd you know Brian?'

'Didn't really, I know Maggie. Been giving her a bit of financial advice,' said Larry, trying to cover up his true relationship with the widow.

'Been sucking her toes?' queried this character before he threw his head back and laughed loudly at his own joke. Larry looked confused before the man explained. 'I was a kid when I first heard the term financial advisor. There was this big scandal because there were pictures in the paper of some geezer sucking Princess Fergie's toes. Supposedly her financial advisor. Didn't quite get the significance at the time but liked the sound of financial advisor, so decided I wanted to be one. Ended up a brickie instead. Done alright too.'

'Oh,' muttered Larry. 'I'm not really officially a financial guy, just a friend who's helping out with sorting out Brian's business. By the way the name's Larry'

'Dominic, nice to meet you, Larry.' They shook hands without spilling Dominic's plate. 'I know you aren't supposed to speak ill of the dead but jeez he was a difficult man to get money out of. Look I always got paid in the end, but never on time. Still l thought it would've been a bit rude not to turn up today, yeah? I've been laying bricks for him on and off for years.'

'He doesn't owe you money now, does he?' asked Larry.

"No, we ended up all square. The Greenacre job is all finished, I think. God, I didn't like the colour of them bricks he chose. l think he was waiting for council approval for his next project. He said he'd need me in a couple of months. Guess that's not gonna happen now.'

Larry was pleased to hear a firsthand account which backed up what the solicitor had said. Perhaps it would be sorted out in time. Maggie had taken him into the heart of Sydney to flog off some of her jewellery for nearly three grand. He was glad he had encouraged her to keep some. She looked beautiful today, in a sad way, in a simple black shift dress enhanced with a real classy gold chain necklace, matching earrings and dark glasses which would have made Jackie Onassis envious. How different her appearance was compared with the dowdy outfit she wore earlier, just a few months ago, to all those funerals. The money from the jewellery plus that found in the freezer would get them back to Melbourne and keep their head above water until some of the business's assets could be sold.

"Guess the cops haven't worked out who did him in, yeah?' said Dominic. 'They're hanging about outside taking photos. They stand out like the proverbial dog's balls; cute blond lass with a middle-aged geezer with cop written all over him. '

'Doesn't worry me,' lied Larry.' I've got nothing to hide. Nasty business. 1 can't imagine what happened.' In the back of Larry's mind doubt still lingered as to whether Henry's mates in Sydney had something to do with it all.

'You know he did have a temper, poor old Brian. It'd got him into strife before.' Dominic looked around the room. 'Anyway, looks like people are making tracks now.' He emptied his stubby and brushed the crumbs off his black chinos. 'Yeah, I'd better go and say a word to his missus. Nice to have met you, Larry.' Once again, they shook hands.

Larry looked around at the handful of mourners and caught sight of the solicitor's blond hair and moved across the room to join him. Shane looked like a man who took funerals seriously, dark suit, black tie, the whole kit.

'Morning Larry. Bit of a disappointing turn out, but 1 guess people lead busy lives.'

'G'day Shane. Just talking to a brickie about Brian's projects and he said the same as you about them,' said Larry before he realised it could be taken the wrong way, 'not that we doubted what you told us.'

'That's okay. I've a bit of news on that front. I have listed the vacant block with an agent who's calling for expressions of interest from developers. We've given them three weeks. The agent thinks we'll have no trouble flogging it off.'

'Sounds good. I'll tell Maggie when she's dealt with this lot.' Larry waved his hand towards the straggling mourners. 'The brickie bloke was saying the cops are outside taking photos.'

'Good luck to them. Can't see his killer turning up here myself. Personally, I reckon his temper has got him in a blue with some random guy.' Shane glanced over at Maggie. 'So, what are your plans?'

'I hope we will be heading back to Melbourne, but it depends on Maggie.'

They discussed how to stay in touch and Shane handed Larry another business card before he ventured over to Maggie to have a word before leaving.

Finally, when everybody had left the funeral ladies kindly suggested they might like to take some of the remaining food with them. A catering lady came from the kitchen with a couple of boxes which they handed to Amanda and Larry. For the first time Maggie laughed much to everybody's confusion except Larry.

'Another funeral eh Maggie. I hope there are some sausage rolls in here,' he said with a grin.

CHAPTER THIRTY-ONE

The throaty engine noise percolated up to flat nine. It was enough to have Gladys spring out of her recliner like a woman many years younger and headed for the venetians. Doctor Phil was unaware that he no longer had her attention. He had already lost Herb's, whose eyes had been closed for some time.

'It's them from number ten back,' she shouted above the noise of the overhead fan and the television. 'Herb, did you hear me, you deaf old coot?'

'Herb!' she shouted once again. Come 'ere and have a look at this.'

Her volume this time resulted in Herb leaving the Hawaiian Islands and returning to the present. 'What do I have to look at now?' he mumbled as he shuffled to the window.

'See, I told you it's that red-headed woman and her fella

from upstairs.'

'Looks like he's got himself a Nissan Patrol. God, that will chew up the juice.' Herb was really more interested in the vehicle than anything else. 'New South plates too. He'll have to change them if he's gonner stay here.'

The SUV had pulled up by the door to the stairwell and the couple were unloading a number of suitcases and cardboard boxes. The woman had some of her clothes on hangers and in those plastic covers you get from the drycleaners, which she took upstairs first.

"Looks like they've been in a good paddock,' observed Gladys. 'She doesn't look as skinny. Suits her don't you reckon?'

'Guess the cops gave her more than bread and water.' joked Herb. 'Perhaps she wasn't a crook after all or else they let her out for Christmas.'

"Why don't you go down Herb and offer to help. You might find out some stuff.'

You're cracked luv. You know I struggle to carry your groceries, much less carry heavy boxes upstairs.' Herb shuffled his way back to his chair.

Gladys had not lost interest and stayed glued to the window, 'How long do you reckon they've been gone Herb? About five weeks? I bet they've been up in Sydney cos that's where her husband's body was found. Was on Crime Stoppers remember? That'd explain the New South plates.' No response came from the old man who just pointed at the noisy overhead fan with one hand while cupping his ear with the other. That was signal enough for Gladys to turn her back on him and continue her surveillance solo.

She watched as the fellow drove the SUV around the back to their allocated parking spot and Mrs. Redhead had returned and started up the stairs with a heavy case. 'I guess they're here for a while,' Gladys said, aware she no longer had an audience and was talking to herself. The bloke returned to the pile of possessions and took off up the stairs with a heavy looking box. Gladys cackled and thought he looked different; perhaps it was the fact he was wearing shorts and shoes without socks. Maybe a bit of Sydney had rubbed off on him. She couldn't imagine her Herb going without socks.

It took the couple the best part of five minutes to carry all their stuff upstairs, allowing Gladys time to study the pair. It seemed that Mrs Redhead was in charge, instructing her man what he should carry up and in what order. Herb would be pleased he was back. The first week he was away, nobody put the rubbish bins out for collection and the following week that job seemed to have fallen on Herb's shoulders. He is far too old to be wheeling heavy bins to the roadside. Hopefully, Mr Sydney, with no socks, will take on looking after the bins. Too many of the other tenants just don't care or are too lazy. The one exception is the Indian bloke in number two who sometimes helps. After everything had been carted upstairs, the show was over. Gladys returned to her chair and Doctor Phil.

CHAPTER THIRTY-TWO

The pub's bistro looked much the same except for the artificial Christmas tree in the far corner. Tinsel was tangled around the jar in the centre of the table that held cutlery and table napkins. Yes, Christmas was only three weeks away.

Larry looked across at Maggie and could not believe his luck. Yesterday she had visited Nicole at the hair salon and now was once again a redhead. Not a grey hair in sight. In his eyes, she looked a million dollars and may soon be worth more than a million dollars. The surprising thing was she still fancied him; in fact, she had suggested that they get married. He had honestly thought her altered financial status might have led to change, but here they were back in Melbourne. Having nothing but himself to offer Maggie, he would never have had the courage to propose to her.

He saw Henry's bulky frame silhouetted at the doorway to the bistro. Henry opened the door for Nicole who led the way to their table in the pub just like when they had first met her. It was two months since he had seen his mate, the last time being when he organised the ride up to Sydney with those flash nags. He stood up to give Nicole a peck on the cheek and shake Henry's hand.

'Good to see you both,' said Larry, surprised when Henry was not happy with just a handshake but grabbed him in a man hug with its conventional back slap.

'Likewise, Prof., thought we would lose you to the bright lights of the harbour city. Guess all that bushfire smoke was too much for you.' Henry switched his eyes to Maggie. 'Boy don't you look a bit of alright,' he said planting a kiss on her cheek and giving her a wink.

Maggie blushed. She was a little self-conscious of her new appearance and was not used to compliments. 'Thanks, Henry, you're too kind. Me and Larry have to thank you for getting him up to Sydney. I don't think I could have managed without him there.'

'So, what are your plans? Are you going back to Sydney or are you going to stay in the world's most liveable city?' asked Henry.

Nicole reached across the table and squeezed the big man's hand. 'Shh for a minute buster, I think Larry wants to ask you something?' She exchanged smiles across the table with Maggie.

Larry was a bit taken back by the direction of the conversation but followed the girls' lead. 'Henry, I need to ask you another favour.'

'What is it Prof? Spit it out and I'll see what I can do,' said Henry, always keen to help.

'Well, mate, I was wondering if you would be me best-man cause Maggie and me are gonna get married.'

Suddenly all eyes in the bistro were on the foursome as Henry bellowed. 'That's bloody fantastic. Congratulations.' He gave Maggie yet another wink. 'Are you sure Maggie? He's a bit of a ratbag.'

'Of course, I'm sure. He might be a ratbag but he's my ratbag. I've already asked Nicole to be best woman or whatever you call bridesmaids these days,' joked Maggie.

'Well, we'd better celebrate with some champers, before we order our tucker. What do you reckon ladies?' Henry was back on his feet.

Larry joined him. 'I'll come with you. By the way, Maggie and me are paying today. We've been freeloading off you long enough.'

'We'll see, you silly bugger,' replied Henry.

They ordered a bottle of Prosecco. While they were waiting for the barmaid to hunt it out Larry was keen to ask Henry about what had been troubling him for the last two months. He just didn't quite know how to broach the subject.

'You know, Larry, the death of Maggie's ex has been the thing that has changed everything, but I still feel a like bit of a prick, being so happy about it,' confessed Larry.

'Don't be daft. You had nothing to do with it; some other bastard sorted him out. The cops worked out who?' Henry eyes were studying the barmaid bending over to get the bottle of sparkling wine.

'Nah, not yet. You didn't speak to your mates in Sydney, did you?'

Henry turned to face Larry. 'Mates in Sydney? I don't know anyone in Sydney other than me Aunty Colleen and a few cousins. Jesus, Prof, I was just bullshitting about mates,' he replied.

But then he did something unusual, making a gesture normally reserved only for the lady folk.

He winked at Larry.

POSTSCRIPT
APRIL 2022

Danny collapsed into a cane chair on his veranda. His run through the streets of Dubbo was becoming part of his daily routine. By choosing a different route each day he was building up his knowledge of his adopted hometown. He pulled out his smart phone that logged the details of his run and checked his stats. Every day, his time was improving.

He cooled down as the early morning sunlight danced its way through the leaves of the lemon scented gum which dominated his front yard. It was an opportunity to check his emails. His shift at the police station did not start for another 90 minutes. He was surprised but pleased to see he had a message from Jess MacDonald.

Hi Danny

Hope things are going well for you in Dubbo and you are happy about moving from the city. I gather from what I have seen on TV and in the news, that Dubbo has had a real tough time with COVID. I can't imagine how it would be having to enforce health regulations. Not what you expect as police work.

You may not have caught up with the news that I have been accepted as a detective. I think that Colin, you remember him, might have pulled a few strings. But then again, I recently graduated with my uni degree with a major in Criminology. Can you believe it? I actually finished. I have attached my graduation photo. Don't my parents look pleased. The good looking one is my younger sister who you might remember was studying nursing. She is qualified now and thinking of doing a stint in the bush. Any jobs going for nurses in Dubbo?

Do let me know how things are turning out.

Jess XX

ACKNOWLEDGMENTS

Many thanks to the members of the writing group to which I belong. The encouragement and advice I have received from Susan Narelle, Philippa, Mel and Lyn has been a huge help in the writing of this book. A special thanks to Susan Narelle who was the one who encouraged me to take up writing.

Thanks also goes to my family for their advice and support.